FALLING FOR THE FORBIDDEN

FORBIDDEN SERIES #1

TRACY LORRAINE

Edited by Pinpoint Editing

Proofread by Literary Luxe Co.

Cover design & formatting by Sammi Bee Designs

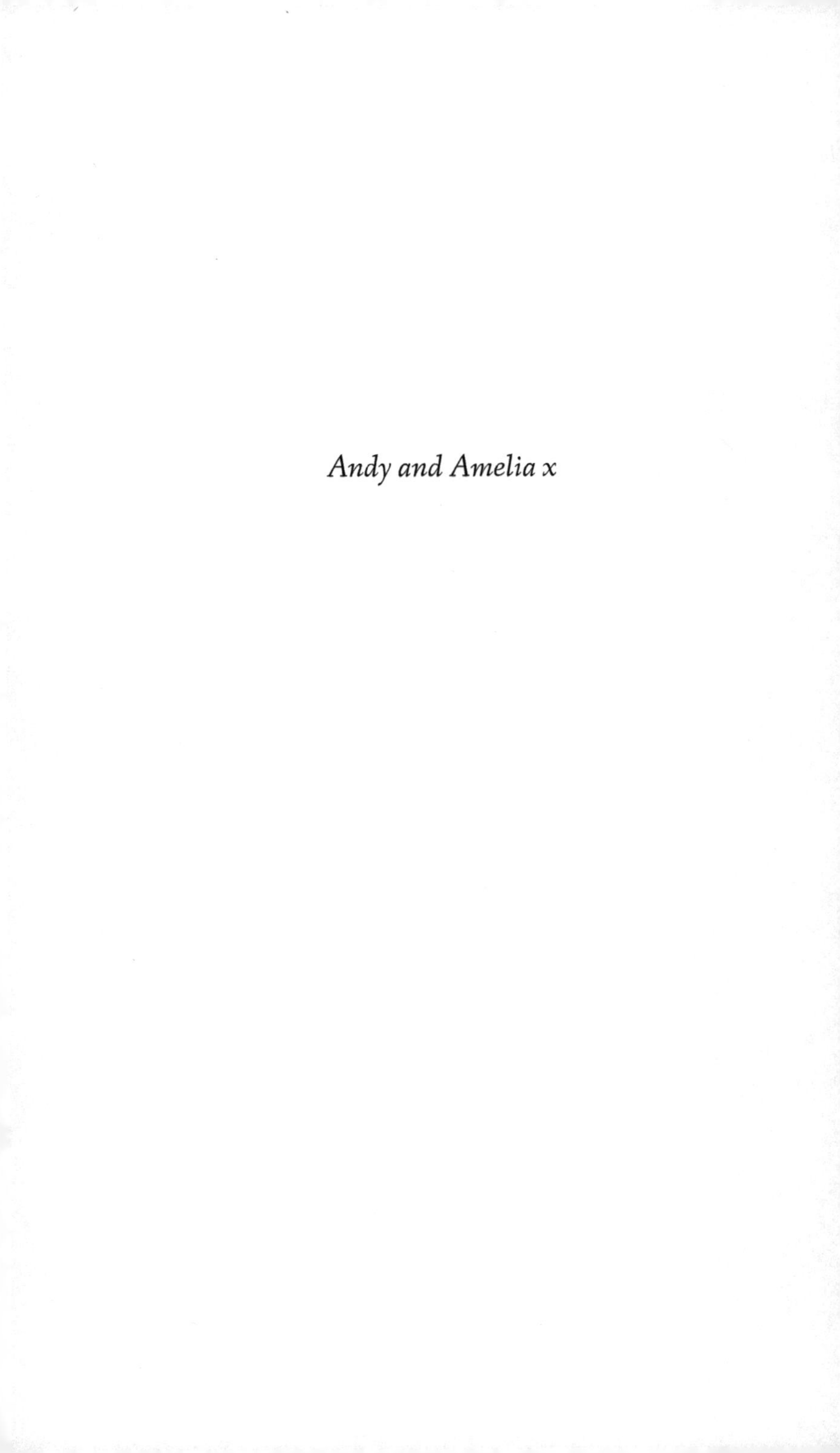

Andy and Amelia x

A NOTE

Falling for the Forbidden is written in British English and contains British spelling and grammar. This may appear incorrect to some readers when compared to US English books.

____

FALLING DOWN ON MY BED, I blow out a long breath and tell myself that everything will be okay.

I had plans for this summer—a few weeks of fun before uni starts. The girls and I had been looking at last-minute holiday deals, and we had tickets for a music festival...but then my dad swooped in, in that way that he does, and ruined everything.

I knew it was coming.

I just wasn't expecting it quite yet.

I'd hoped agreeing to study what he wanted me to and working for him was enough—apparently not.

I decided a few years ago that I wasn't going to move away to study. I mostly love my life in London, and I loved living with Mum. I'm not ashamed to admit that she's one of my best friends. It was only as I started looking at universities that my dad piped up and told me that I would be studying accountancy and finance at The London School of Economics. He'd done his research and decided it was the best place for me to learn my trade so I could enter the family business.

I just about managed to contain my laughter when he emphasised the word *family*.

I've no idea how long I lie on my bed trying to convince myself that moving into his house with his new wife and her son isn't the worst thing to ever happen to me, but eventually my stomach rumbling has me moving. I sit on the edge of the bed and take in all my half-unpacked boxes. A large sigh falls from my lips. If I don't find everything a home, maybe I won't have to stay. I know it's wishful thinking. This is it for me now.

Disappointment floods me as I make my way through the silent house. It's not that I was expecting a welcome party or anything, but someone being here would have been nice. Someone to help me carry everything up to my room would have been even nicer. Since Dad moved in with Jenny a few years ago, I've been told to treat this place like my home.

It will never be.

It's just a house, a show home, a shell in which I'm scared to touch anything for fear of making a mess. Home is a place with character, with mess from day-to-day living, with people who love and care for you.

My dad isn't a bad man, per se, but he's not exactly what you'd describe as a doting father. Everything he does is for his own gain—if it happens to help others in the process, that's just a bonus.

My step mum, Jenny, is lovely. She really is, but I can't help feeling like she's just a little bit...broken. She makes all the right comments and does all the right things. She's a great mum. But there's such sadness in her eyes.

The fridge is full, as usual. It's strange, because I've never witnessed anyone eating more than a slice of toast or an apple in this kitchen.

I fix myself a salad with the unopened packets of fruit and vegetables, but it doesn't really have the effect I needed it to have. Being here makes me feel kind of empty, and no amount of lettuce leaves is going to fill the void after moving out of the flat Mum and I shared for the past few years.

Rummaging through the cupboards, I can't help smiling when I find a stash of naughty stuff hiding at the back.

Pulling my hair back into a messy bun, I put my thoughts to the side and set about making something that will make me feel just a little bit better.

The sun's just about to set, casting an orange

glow throughout the kitchen. It almost makes it feel warm and inviting—almost. My mouth waters as I pour melted chocolate over the crushed biscuits and marshmallows I've managed not to eat already. Standing in only a vest and a small pair of hot pants, I decide to make myself a hot chocolate, grab a blanket, and enjoy my bowl of goodness out on the deck with a magazine. Chocolate makes everything that little bit better. If I eat enough, it might make me forget what this summer's actually going to be like for me.

I'm just waiting for the kettle to boil when a shiver runs down my spine. I'm sure it's just the size of the house that freaks me out. I've seen enough horror films to know there are plenty of hiding places in a place this big.

I'm still for a second, but when I don't hear anything, I continue with what I was doing. That is, until a deep rumbling voice has every nerve in my body on alert.

"Wow, step daddy sure is attracting the young ones these days." His voice is slurred, his anger palpable. It makes goosebumps prick my skin and a giant lump form in my throat. "You look too pure. Too innocent to be with that prick," he spits.

There's no love lost between my dad and my stepbrother, that's not news to me, but the viciousness of his voice right now makes me wonder what their relationship is really like. My dad might be many things, but he wouldn't cheat on Jenny—he loves her too much.

I can't remember the last time I saw him, but there's no way he can't know it's me. Who the hell else would be cooking in his kitchen? Deciding he's just trying to rile me up, I go to collect my stuff and get out of his way. Unfortunately, he seems to have other ideas.

His breath tickles up my neck moments before the heat of his body warms my back.

"You came here for the wrong man. I can put that right, though." The alcohol on his breath surrounds me. It's a reminder that there's a good chance he has no idea what he's doing right now.

The softness of his nose running up the length of my neck has tingles racing through my traitorous body. I don't realise he's smelling me until he blows out a long breath and the scent of alcohol hits me once again. I turn to leave, but his hands slam on the counter behind me and cage me in.

"Look at me," he demands.

"Let me go, Ben."

If he's surprised to discover it's me, he doesn't show it. If anything, his eyes shine with delight as he takes in every inch of my face before focusing on my lips. My stomach flips, knowing where his thoughts are.

Something passes over his face but it's gone too quickly to be able to identify. He pushes himself from the counter and away from me. No more words are said, but when he gets to the door, he looks back over his shoulder and runs his eyes over my body. They hold a warning I don't really understand.

Once he's disappeared from sight, I sag back against the counter. What the hell was that?

After putting half of the rocky road on a tray in the fridge, I forgo sitting outside and instead take my spoils to my room to hide. There's stuff everywhere in my room and, unlike the rest of this house, it makes me feel a little more relaxed.

Since the day Ben and I were introduced by our parents, we've not really had any kind of relationship. He's pretty much stayed out of my way and, in turn, I've done the same. It's not all that much of a task. When I'm here, he spends almost every minute somewhere else. When he's home, he's moody, arrogant, and generally a prick, so I'm more than happy to stay out of his way.

It's just a shame he's so damn pretty to look at. As the years have passed, he's only become more attractive, too. I've no idea if it's just his job or if he works out as well because every inch of him seems to be toned to perfection.

Jenny spends most of her time apologising for his attitude and trying to explain that he's got a lot going on. I'm yet to discover what that is. As far as I can tell, he seems to be your average twenty-year-old guy who'd rather be off his arse drunk or with a woman than spending time at home with his parents.

By the time I've dug my way to the bottom of the bowl, I feel pretty sick. There's still no sign of my dad or Jenny, but the music pounding from Ben's room across the hallway leaves no doubt as to what kind of mood he's in.

CHAPTER TWO

THE STEADY BEAT of Ben's music must have eventually sent me to sleep, because the next thing I know, the sun is streaming in through the crack in the curtains and everything's silent once again.

After freshening myself up, I drag the hoodie I stole from my ex over my head, suddenly aware of just how much skin I had on display last night, and go in search of a cup of tea.

Just like the night before, everything is silent. There are no signs of them returning home late last night...no shoes by the door or a dirty glass in the kitchen sink like normal people. The whole place is, once again, perfect. Even the mess I made in the kitchen is gone, like I never existed.

Dad and Jenny eventually show their faces, going directly for the coffee machine. Dad mutters a good morning before disappearing into his office. I know that his argument for me living here was so I could be close for both work and uni, but I've not even been here twenty-four hours yet, and I'm pretty sure no one would have noticed if I hadn't bothered. I shouldn't really be shocked that Dad just wants me to fall neatly into his perfectly planned-out life, but I guess I am. When he originally suggested it, I was ready to point-blank refuse, but Mum seemed to think it was an excellent idea. I must remember to thank her for pushing this on me the next time I speak to her.

"Can you make sure you're free Sunday night? The four of us are going out to celebrate you moving in and officially starting at Johnson & Sons," Jenny asks once she's had a sip of her coffee.

The idea fills me with dread, but I agree before she also disappears. I hear her talking to someone before the house goes silent once again.

I'm still poking cereal around in a bowl when the atmosphere in the room changes. I don't need to look up to know why, but I do, nonetheless.

My breath catches at the sight of him. His dark hair sticks up in all directions, and his eyes are red and bloodshot, dark circles surrounding them.

"Morning," I sing politely.

All I get in response is a grunt and an angry

glance as he follows in the steps of our parents and kicks the coffee machine into action. The scent of the beans once again fills the room and, just like always, I turn my nose up. I've no idea how anyone can drink that vile stuff.

AFTER FLICKING through the channels on my TV, I let out a long sigh. It's the first day of what should be my summer holiday, and I'm fed up already.

Grabbing my phone, I send a message to my best friend, Danni, who took me under her wing on my first day of sixth form and showed me the ropes. We hit it off instantly and have been close ever since, despite our obvious differences. She lives in an incredible house in Chelsea with her parents, whereas I was on the outskirts of the city in a small two-bedroom flat with Mum. Thankfully, her family don't see money quite the way Dad does. They're the most down-to-earth people I've ever met, despite the millions they've made from their antiques business.

It doesn't take much convincing for Danni to persuade me to stay at her place and go out for cocktails. I've only been here one night and I already can't wait to get out.

"SO, HOW'S THE SHOW HOME?" she asks as we're getting ready.

"About a fun as expected." Dropping my eyeliner pencil, I glance at Danni, sitting on her bed with a cocktail at her lips, her eyes filled with sympathy. "I'm sure it'll only get better once I start work on Monday."

"I can't believe you've got to work *all* summer. Zante won't be the same without you." My heart drops at her words. Our group of friends has spent months planning our first holiday without our parents—not to mention that I saved my arse off to be able to afford to go. But Dad put pay to any plans I had the moment he told me what my summer would consist of.

"You'll have an amazing time." I try to put as much excitement into my voice as possible, but I don't think I really manage it.

"I guess," she says sadly. "Anyway, how is it, living with Ben?" Her eyebrows wiggle in interest. It's no secret that not a single one of my friends would say no to a night with my stepbrother. His reputation still preceded him when I started at the same school he went to. It helped me fit in, in a sense, but it also made me a target for any girls brave enough to want to find out more about the elusive bad boy.

"He's..." The couple of interactions I've had with him run through my mind as I try to come up with a suitable answer. "Interesting."

"Interesting? That's all you've got?" Shrugging, I go back to finishing off my make-up.

The night is exactly as it should be. We drink, dance, and flirt with a group of guys who spend most of the night buying us drinks. I forget about what's on the horizon and just enjoy being eighteen while I still can.

We don't stumble back to Danni's house until almost dawn, and we sleep until well past lunch.

Her mum takes pity on our fragile states when we eventually emerge from Danni's bedroom and makes us bacon sandwiches to help cure our hangovers. Sadly, it doesn't even take the edge off mine.

I'm still feeling the effects of the previous night's over-indulgence and lack of sleep when I push the key into the lock of my new home later that day. The driveway's empty when the taxi drops me off, aside from my car, and the house is empty. Rolling my eyes, I slip my flip-flops off then carry them and my overnight bag up to my room.

I SPEND what's left of the day hiding in my room, watching films. I've no desire to venture downstairs and put on the act everyone else seems to. I can hear Dad and Jenny talking in the distance and eventually they come up to bed before the sound of their voices fades away.

I just start to drift off when the sound of the doorbell startles me. I wait to hear if there's going to be any movement, but other than the echo from the ringing, it stays silent.

My curiosity gets the better of me and I walk to the window to see if they're still at the door.

When I don't see anyone, I go to drop the curtain and get back in bed, but something catches my eye at the last minute. Someone is slumped in front of the house. I don't need to use too much brainpower to figure out that it's Ben.

Grabbing the hoodie I left hanging over the chair by the window, I pull it on and make my way down to rescue him.

"Ben?" He doesn't move or show any signs that he's aware of my presence. "Ben?" I say a little louder, but it's not until I bend down and give his shoulder a shake that I get any response.

"Yeah? What?" His voice is slurred and rough.

"Let's get you inside. Can you stand?"

"Of course I can fucking stand. I don't need your help," he snaps, trying to push himself up from the floor and falling straight back down.

"Oh, really?" I can't help but laugh at him. When he looks up at me, his face is hard, but his eyes show his own amusement. Maybe he's not quite as drunk as I first thought.

With the help of the wall, he stands to his full height. He towers above me at well over six feet tall, making me feel tiny. I'm not sure how much help I'll be, but I wrap my arm around his waist anyway.

A jolt of electricity shoots through me at our contact, and I immediately feel his eyes staring down at me.

Refusing to look up and acknowledge whatever just sparked between us, I focus on getting him inside.

"I really am okay," he says, his voice suddenly sounding much steadier than only moments ago. "You don't need to look after me."

"I'm just looking out for you."

"Why? No one else bothers."

My heart drops at his words. I'm saddened that what I experience in this house is his life. At least I have my mum at the other end of the phone if I need an ear to listen or a shoulder to cry on.

"I—"

Ben places large hands on my shoulders and turns me to look at him. A similar sensation rushes through me as it did when I first touched him.

I expect him to snap again. It seems to be his go-to defence mechanism whenever I've attempted to get close to him in the past, so I'm surprised when his eyes soften. "Thank you," he whispers.

Just when I think that maybe we're getting somewhere, his features harden once again, his mask goes back on, and he turns away from me.

He only makes it up two stairs before he falls flat on his face.

Silently laughing at his drunken state, I once again go to help him. To my surprise, he allows me to attempt to get him up the stairs, although I'm pretty sure he's just humouring me.

We come to a stop at his bedroom door. I remove my arm from around his waist and go to step away, but my breath comes out in a rush when I'm forcefully pulled back to him. My breasts press against his chest, and his heat burns through the fabric between us.

"Is that hoodie your boyfriend's?"

"Huh?"

"That hoodie you're wearing. It's a guy's."

"Oh. Yeah."

"Boyfriend?" he repeats.

"No. It's...it's my ex's," I stutter. The look he's giving me makes me nervous.

"Ex?"

"We weren't a very good match." His eyebrow lifts and I can't help more falling from my lips. "He wanted things I...wasn't ready for."

"Fuck," he barks, his features hardening as understanding dawns. I expect him to push me away but he only pulls me tighter against him. My heart thunders in my chest as his eyes continue to bore down into mine. He must be able to feel my body trembling against his, but he doesn't react.

"Ben?" I ask when the silence continues to stretch between us.

His eyes flick down to my lips when his name falls from them. I'm powerless to stop my tongue running along my bottom lip in anticipation. When he does eventually move, I find myself stumbling across the hallway.

The slam of his door vibrates through the entire house. I feel it in the wall at my back. It's the only evidence I have that what just happened wasn't my imagination. My racing heart and quivering body sure point towards it all being real.

He was going to kiss me, I'm sure of it.

Why me, and why now? He's gone out of his way

to avoid me since our parents forced us on each other. He's been nothing but an arsehole.

After a few seconds of confusion, the sound of another door closing has me moving. I push myself from the wall and make my way back to my room.

***

"LAUREN? BEN? ARE YOU READY?" Dad hollers up the stairs.

I've no idea where we're going for this meal, but I'm assuming it's somewhere pretentious to make Dad look good. I'm wearing a pencil skirt and a blouse instead of the jeans and vest I really want to be in.

"Just coming," I call back before swiping some gloss over my lips and smoothing down my hair.

"You look beautiful, sweetheart," Dad says when I get to the bottom step. Seeing him in a suit and Jenny in a floral summer dress makes me think my assumption might be spot on. He's much less impressed when Ben eventually makes an appearance. "What the fuck is that?" he barks, making both Jenny and I turn towards the stairs.

He's wearing a pair of ripped jeans and a white V-neck, skin-tight t-shirt. "What?"

"Go and put some decent clothes on."

"These *are* decent."

The two of them stare at each other, a silent argument raging between them.

"Ben, please," Jenny begs, stepping in before things kick off. "Just go and put a shirt on, at least."

"This is a fucking joke," he mutters as he disappears up the stairs. I can't help but agree with him. This whole 'let's be a family' thing all of a sudden is a bit much. I'm actually surprised he even agreed to it in the first place. He usually avoids any family event at all costs.

The drive towards the restaurant is silent and awkward as fuck as Ben and I sit beside each other in the back. His words from the night before and the feel of his body pressed against mine are still at the forefront of my mind, but now we're out as a *family*, it makes everything I'm still feeling seem very, very wrong.

From the moment we sit down at our table, Dad has his phone out. He's totally oblivious to the death stares he keeps getting from Jenny.

"So, Lauren, are you looking forward to starting work tomorrow?"

"Uh...yeah, I think so. I'm a little nervous."

"Aww, no need for that. Everyone's lovely. Right, Ben?"

"Yeah, great. The boss is a bit of a dick, though." I can't help but snort a laugh.

"Ben, don't," Jenny snaps, but Dad's too focused on whatever he's doing to have heard.

The waiter comes over to take our orders and Dad actually looks surprised when we prompt him to say what he wants. His eyes scan the menu quickly before ordering a steak and being pissed off when he's asked how he'd like it cooked.

"Who in their right mind would order it any way other than rare in a place like this?" he grumbles once the waiter's left us to it.

"Let's just enjoy our evening. Work keeps us busy all week."

"This won't wait. Unless you want to deal with it?" Dad snaps at Jenny, who pales at his outburst.

"No, no. You know what you're doing. Just don't spend all night on that thing." The glare she receives would make most people cower, but somehow, she manages to hold her own.

Looking back to the two of us, she continues with her earlier small talk. I don't need to see him; I can sense the tension radiating from Ben because of the way my dad talks to his mum. Thankfully, he has enough self-control to keep his disapproval to himself —for now, at least.

Dad's phone rings and he immediately answers it before getting up and walking out of the restaurant to deal with whatever is so important on a Sunday night.

"I'm just going to use the bathroom before the food arrives," Jenny whispers, watching her husband disappear from sight.

"Well, this is fun," Ben says once we're alone.

"That's one way to describe it. I'm surprised you turned up."

"There's...suddenly something worth making the effort for." His eyes drop from mine, to my lips, and then lower. My whole body heats under his gaze and I squirm in my seat. "You're fucking trouble." It's the last thing he says before Dad reappears, looking pissed off. Ben goes back to sitting mutely beside me for the rest of the meal, but I don't miss the odd glance my way when Dad's distracted.

Once the bill's paid, we rush out of there like the place is on fire. Jenny looks upset, and I feel bad for her...but I fear she's trying to turn us all into something we're never going to be.

A perfect family.

CHAPTER THREE

I'VE NO IDEA WHY, but as I walk into the office for my first day, I'm nervous as hell. I've been here many times, and I've met every single person, but still, butterflies continue to riot in my belly. I put it down to the fact my dad's about to become my boss, and I know exactly what everyone around here thinks of him. I don't expect special treatment because I'm his daughter, but I do hope for a little reprieve from him.

I follow Dad as he barks instructions at Betty and Erica, who are sitting at their desks, ready to start the week. Betty immediately jumps up and rushes towards the kitchen to make Dad his morning coffee.

"Would you like anything, sweetheart?" she asks when she spots me.

"Uh...tea would be great. Thank you."

Betty has been working for Johnson & Sons for so long that she's practically part of the furniture. I think before my dad took up residence in the office and started throwing his weight around, she was probably classed as one of the family. But Dad's done a stellar job of turning this friendly family business into something more corporate. His desire to be the best knows no bounds, and the second he could get his teeth into this place, he did.

Pushing the nagging feeling that this business is the only reason Dad married Jenny to the back of my mind, I walk over to my desk. I worked here for a few weeks last summer so I know my way around. I mostly spent those weeks doing menial tasks like shredding, but this time, I'm an actual employee with actual responsibilities. I'm not sure whether I should be excited or scared.

"Are you ready for this?" Erica asks. We hit it off immediately last year. She'd just dropped out of uni and found herself an admin job here. Thankfully, she's got plenty of backbone and can handle herself around my dad.

"Honestly, I've no idea."

"It'll be fine. You're up for tonight, right?"

"What's happening tonight?"

Rolling her eyes at me like I shouldn't even need to ask, she says, "Your new job drinks."

"Oh...uh...it's okay."

"No, no it's not. It's tradition for any new staff—*under the age of about...thirty-five,*" she whispers, "to go out for drinks on their first day."

"Even on a Monday?"

"This is London, hon. Every night is Friday night."

I grin. "Okay, then. When and where?"

"The Olive Branch. Eight o'clock. To start with."

"To start with?"

"Oh, honey, you've no idea."

My first day is exhausting, and not just because I only had a few hours sleep the night before. My hopes for being eased in gently were dashed the second I was given accounts to go over, customers to contact, and invoices to process. Being a member of the 'family' means I get access to everything.

Dad's mentioned the day I take over the company more than once since I moved in. To begin with, I corrected him, saying that Ben was the one who would one day own it, seeing as it's actually *his* family business, but I was soon put in my place. He seems to think that, by marrying Jenny, he's entitled to everything. Which I guess is true. Once again, I question his intentions, but I push the thoughts aside every time they pop up because, although my dad might not be winning any parenting awards anytime soon, I like to believe he's pretty genuine and just wants to be successful.

WALKING INTO THE OLIVE BRANCH, I pull at my dress, questioning my choice when I see that most people around me are still in their work clothes. I look around for Erica or any of the others I might recognise from work, but I before I find them, I hear my name being shouted.

Following the sound, I find Erica waving like a loon from her spot by the bar. As I walk over, I get a better view of what she's wearing. Her silver dress sits high on her thighs and the back is completely missing. Suddenly, I don't feel self-conscious at all about my slightly revealing red wrap dress.

"Wow, Lauren. Look at you. The guys are going to trip over themselves!"

"I'm sure that'll go down well with my Dad," I say with a laugh I don't really feel.

The bar soon fills up, and it's not long before the sounds of a large group of guys filter through to us.

"Oh, they're here. Are you ready for this?"

My stomach drops. I hadn't realised when Erica invited me earlier that we'd be the only females, but I guess it was obvious seeing as we work for a building company and all the other women in the office are above her thirty-five age limit to be invited. We're pretty outnumbered.

The second they get to us, Erica is pulled into Will's arms before he spins her around, getting a good look at her exposed skin. "Looking good tonight, gorgeous," he growls, his pupils growing darker by the second. Until he looks up and spots me. "Wait a fucking minute. Is this little Lauren?" My cheeks heat and my skin prickles as he runs his eyes over every inch of me. My hands clench with the need to do something to put an end to his molestation. I've no idea what it is, but something about Will creeps me out.

"Dude," a familiar voice barks before Will lifts his hand to rub his head where he was just slapped.

"What? Just fucking look at her." Something erupts inside me when Ben appears from behind him. His eyes run the length of me and, unlike the unwelcome feeling of Will's attention, my body erupts in goosebumps. "Anyway, it's not like she's your actual sister."

Ben has Will's shirt in his fist in seconds, their noses almost touching. He drops his voice so low, I have no chance of hearing what he says. But whatever it is, it works, because Will does apologise to me the minute he's released.

Thankfully, he turns his attention back to Erica. Once we've all got a drink, I'm introduced to some of the guys I've yet to meet. I get hungry eyes from a few of them, but the moment Erica reveals who my father is, they soon lose interest. I can understand why.

Ben says nothing to me. Instead, he stays with some of the guys at the other side of our group. That doesn't mean I don't feel his eyes burning into me every few minutes. I fight the need to look up, too afraid of my body's reaction if I catch him staring.

We have a couple of rounds of drinks before Erica rounds everyone up to head towards a club.

"It's a Monday night," I complain when she links arms with me and steers me towards the exit.

"And?"

I guess if I'm going to be starting uni in a few weeks, I'd better get used to this kind of nightlife. "Nothing. Where are we going?"

"Just wait, you're going to love it!"

The club, Erica's favourite, is called Fire, and it's insane. I've no idea how many floors there are, but we came up at least three sets of stairs to get to the bar we're currently stood at, waiting for drinks.

"Two rum and Cokes, six pints, and eight shots of...Apple Sourz, please," Erica shouts at the bartender.

In minutes, I'm holding a drink in each hand as I watch all the others down their shots. I follow suit and wince when the sour liquid makes my mouth water.

"And that one, hon," Erica says, nodding to my rum and Coke. "It's time to dance."

Draining the glass as quickly as I can, I allow Erica to pull me towards the crowded dance floor. We're only alone for one song before a few of the guys join us. Jon pulls Erica to him and they start grinding against one another before I feel hands on my waist.

My skin prickles, so I'm not surprised to find Will when I turn around and remove myself from his grip. Pouting, he tries to grab me again but, before he reaches me, his hands are slapped away and another body blocks him from me.

"We're leaving," Ben barks, grabbing my forearm to pull me away.

"Why?" I stand firm. I already have to follow Dad's orders. I refuse to have another man trying to control my life.

"Because you're drunk, and Will's a dick."

"And you're not? You're the one ruining my fun."

"Lauren," he growls.

"Don't *Lauren* me. I'm having fun. How about you dance with me instead?" I step into his personal space, his body heat burning the front of me. He stills, his eyes boring down into mine. "What? You don't dance?"

"I can dance just fine. Let's go." With his hands on my waist, he guides me from the dance floor and then the club.

Once we step outside and the coldness of the night hits me, I realise I'm too drunk and exhausted to start arguing with him. With his hand still resting on my lower back, he finds us a taxi and we head for home.

The house is in darkness when we enter. Leaving Ben in the hallway, I start to weave my way up the stairs, knowing I really need to get to sleep if I'm ever going to make it to day two of my job.

"Lauren, wait," he calls when I'm halfway up. "Let me help you."

With his arm wrapped around my waist, he helps guide me towards my room. I might be tipsy, but I'm not too drunk to manage myself. The feeling of his solid body pressed up against mine is too good, though, so I allow him to continue. I guess he owes me, anyway, after the other night.

Pushing my bedroom door open, he comes to a stop. "You okay from here?"

When I look up at him, I find dark, hungry eyes

staring down at me. His lips are pressed into a thin line and there's a rapid pulse throbbing in his neck.

Finding his eyes once again, the silence between us stretches out. That is, until the sound of the toilet flushing from the other end of the house reaches us.

"Fuck. I need to...Damn it."

I don't get a chance to question him, because he's gone and his bedroom door is closed behind him.

THE WEEK FLIES by once I manage to rid myself of Monday night's hangover. As Friday comes towards an end, I can't wait for the weekend to start. I have no plans as of yet, but that's fine, because right now, all I want to do is sleep.

I'm just finishing up going through last month's invoices when I spot something. Dad's already been through them once, and he told me there was no need for me to do so as well, but it helps me understand the process. Now, I'm here, and I might as well make the most of the opportunity, even if I'm not sure I want to spend the rest of my life working with numbers like he assumes.

Everyone else in the office has left for the day, so when I come across something that looks wrong and doesn't add up, I've got no one to ask. I go over it again and again, but I can't figure it out.

Where the hell could fifty thousand pounds have gone?

Eventually, I shut my computer down for the night in frustration. I hate not knowing everything, but with only a few days under my belt, I've got a lot to learn and the answer is probably staring me right in the face.

Unsurprisingly, the house is deserted when I get home. Ben's probably out getting pissed like he is most weekends. I've no idea where Dad and Jenny are, but they seem to make a hobby out of trying to spend as little time at home as possible.

I've barely seen Ben since the night he helped me up to my room. That makes it easier to pretend that what happened between us is just a very vivid part of my imagination.

Seeing as it's Friday night, I run myself a bath and order a takeaway for when I get out. I'd hoped to spend tonight catching up with Mum, but when I rang her yesterday to make plans, she excitedly reminded me about her weekend away with her sister. We still talk almost daily, but damn, I miss her.

The discrepancy on the accounts still nags at me while I lie surrounded by bubbles. I do my best to push it aside and relax. Turning up my favourite playlist on my phone, I sink down into the warm water.

I FEEL REFRESHED when I wake up late Saturday morning. As I lie in bed, considering what I want to spend the day doing, I'm amazed that I can hear chatting in the house. My curiosity has me getting out of bed and dressed to find out if this family could be doing something as normal as having breakfast together.

I'm wrong, of course. As I get closer to the kitchen, I realise that what I thought was light chitchat is actually a heated argument. Jenny sits at the island, mute, while Dad and Ben argue about responsibilities and appropriate behaviour. The second I join them, they stop what they're doing. Jenny looks at me and apologies for the noise—I swear all she does is apologise for other people. Dad and Ben continue staring daggers at each other until Ben storms from the room and out the back door.

"He'll come to his senses, love," Jenny says softly, placing her arm on Dad's forearm, but it does little to calm the fire raging in his eyes.

"You keep saying that, but all he does is disobey the rules."

"He's just struggling at the moment."

"He's a twenty-year-old man, Jenny. He needs to grow up," Dad spits out. If Jenny is surprised by his outburst, she doesn't show it.

They take their seats around the table and silently sip on their coffees. The tension surrounding them is almost palpable, and I consider turning on my heels and walking straight out of the house to get away from it all. Mum's flat is empty. I could spend the weekend there in peace.

I'm starting to fully understand why Ben's never home.

"Would you like some breakfast, darling?" Jenny asks me, her voice sickly sweet. I know she's trying to make up for my dad's attitude, but it's really not necessary. His temper isn't news to me.

I agree and sit myself beside Dad, who's still tense, while Jenny floats around the kitchen. I watch them both, trying to figure them out. I never noticed before, but since moving in with them, the cracks in their relationship are obvious. I still think they genuinely love each other, but there's some strange kind of tension between them, almost like they're trying too hard.

Thinking it might take Dad's mind off whatever was going on with Ben, I bring up what I thought I found with the accounts yesterday.

"You're wrong," Dad barks the second I suggest I couldn't account for fifty grand.

"Probably," I admit, "but I'd really like to go over it with you so I can—"

"Enough, Lauren. I didn't give you a job so you could question everything I do. I just need you to do your damn job. Is that too much to ask?" A lump forms in my throat and tears sting my eyes. I feel like a child under his intense, angry stare. "What the hell is wrong with the kids in this house? You've both had everything you could ever desire, yet you're totally incapable of doing the most simple of tasks."

My lip trembles and I'm about to interrupt to apologise when warm fingers circle my wrist. Sucking in a breath, I'm pulled up and into a solid wall of man. I recognise his scent immediately.

Before I know what's happening, I find myself in the passenger seat of his BMW with him jogging around to the driver's side.

As he reverses off the drive, I get my first chance to look at him. Sweat beads his brow, his hair's a little damp and curling out from his neck, his skin's flushed, and his chest is heaving. His black t-shirt clings to his body like a second skin, showing off every muscle covering his solid frame.

"Stop it," he snaps, startling me.

"Stop what?"

"Running your eyes over me like that."

"Wh—I...uh...was wondering what's going on."

"Do you always let him talk to you like that?"

"No. He—"

"Do not make excuses for him, Lauren." The way my name sounds coming from his lips has my insides clenching. He's angry, his white-knuckle grip on the wheel shows that, but his voice is also deeper, rougher than usual.

"I...uh...I wasn't," I argue, and he gives me a look, casting a glance over at me that tells me he knows I'm lying. "What? I shouldn't have questioned him."

"Why not?"

"Because he's right. I don't really know what I'm talking about."

"Says who?"

"Him and everyone who's worked for Johnson & Sons for longer than me, I would imagine."

"It doesn't mean you're wrong. Trust your gut, Lauren. If you think something's wrong, it probably is."

"Just like being alone with you feels dangerous?"

His eyes flash with something. Excitement, shock, I'm not sure. It's not until I see his reaction that I realise I said those words out loud.

"Dangerous?" he repeats, intrigue filling his voice.

"Uh...yeah...anyone ever tell you you're a shit driver?"

His laugh lightens the atmosphere in the car. It's like I can breathe properly for the first time since being pushed inside it. "No, no one's ever told me that."

"First time for everything," I mutter quietly. I'm not expecting an answer, so I jump a little when I hear his voice.

"I guess there is."

I've no idea if it's meant to be, but it feels like a promise. My thighs clench and my cheeks flush with embarrassment. "You okay?" When I risk a look, he's got a sexy little smirk playing on his lips.

Damn him.

"Yeah. I'm good. Thanks. What were you and my dad arguing about?"

Blowing out a long breath, he considers his answer. "It would probably be quicker to go through the things we don't argue about."

"Oh?" I knew they didn't really see eye-to-eye, but I didn't realise things between them were that bad.

"It's nothing you need to worry about."

"No, but you can tell me anyway."

"He just...doesn't agree with my choices."

"What choices?"

"All of them." Pulling the car to a stop, he looks over at me. His face is softer than I'm used to seeing, but it's clear his walls are built right up. There's no way I'm breaking them down anytime soon, if ever. Not that I'm sure I want to. "No one deserves to be dragged into my life."

"You're forgetting something."

"I am?"

"Like it or not, I'm part of your life. I'm already in it. So what's the harm in sharing the load?"

"Motherfucker," he mutters, but it's with a smile twitching at the corners of his mouth. "Things aren't always what they appear to be. Let's just leave it at that."

I open my mouth to question his cryptic statement, but before I get a chance to say anything, he's out of the car and shutting his door behind him.

For the first time since he came to a stop, I look out the window and focus on where he's brought us. The park.

"Ben, what are—oh!" I can't help but laugh as I watch him lift a picnic basket from the boot of his car. It's wicker and has red and white gingham fabric poking out from the edge. It's the last thing I think I ever expected to see him carrying.

With my eyebrows raised in surprise, I look up at him.

"I was meant to be meeting friends for a picnic," he says with a shrug.

"Y—you should go. Don't change your plans for me."

"Lauren," he says, stopping and turning his angry eyes on me. I suck in a breath at their intensity, but I know it isn't directed at me. "There isn't anywhere else I'd rather be."

My lips form an O and I fall into step beside him.

With the basket in one hand and a blanket tucked under his arm, he places his other hand at the small of my back and guides me towards the vast expanse of grass beyond.

We come to a stop under a huge oak tree and Ben shakes out the blanket before placing the basket in the middle and lying down next to it.

"I won't bite," he says when he looks up and sees I'm still standing.

"I'm not sure I believe that." My voice comes out as an unsure whisper and he doesn't miss it.

"Remember what I said about trusting your gut." He winks at me and I fall down onto my back, allowing the sun peeking through the leaves to warm my skin.

I feel heat coming from somewhere else, and when I turn my head and crack one eye open, I find Ben staring down at me.

"You're really beautiful."

Propping myself up on my elbows, I look around to see who he's talking to. We're still alone, and heat blooms from my cheeks, warming down my neck. Slowly, I look over to find him staring right at me.

"You're talking to me?"

"No, that tree over there. Of course I'm talking to you." I fight to keep my eyes on his, but his stare gets too intense and I have to look away. "Hey..." His warm fingertips connect with my jaw and my head is gently turned so I have no choice but to look back up at him. His deep blue eyes hold a sincerity I don't think I've ever seen before.

He's silent for the longest time. When he does speak, it's not to say any of the things I imagined might fall from his mouth.

"Fancy a sausage roll?"

CHAPTER FOUR

ONCE I STOP LAUGHING, our conversation takes a bit of a lighter note. We steer clear of bringing up anything to do with work or our parents.

I never thought I'd say it, but I end up having an amazing day with Ben. He's still intense and brooding, but as time goes on, he manages to let go of some of the anger that seems to follow him around and, for the first time since we were introduced, I feel like I've actually got to know him a little. He's not nearly as scary as I once thought he was. That fear has been replaced by another feeling, one I'm not all that comfortable thinking about.

The way he looks at me, the gentleness of his touch—he awakens things within me that I've not experienced before, and that can't be a good thing.

I had a semi-serious boyfriend last year. I enjoyed

my time with him, but I didn't feel the pull I do when I'm with Ben. The more time I spend with him, the more I seem to crave his attention...and his touch.

"Lauren, is that you?" Dad calls out the second we step foot inside the house.

"Yeah, Dad. I'll be right there."

"Don't take any of his bullshit. I'll be upstairs if you need me." Ben's fingers brush against mine and he squeezes quickly before disappearing up the stairs, leaving me with the tingles kickstarted by his caress.

"Lauren?" Dad snaps.

Following the sound of his voice, I find him in his office, staring at a spreadsheet.

"I wanted to go through what you thought you saw yesterday so we don't have the same misunderstanding again."

"Oh. Yeah, sure." Pulling up a chair, I silently listen as Dad talks through the spreadsheet and the figures on it. He does the same calculation I did the previous day...and the total is fifty thousand pounds more than what I worked out.

"See, everything's fine. You must have missed something."

"Yeah. I guess so."

"Happy now?"

I mumble my agreement, but Ben's words linger

in my mind. *Trust your gut, Lauren. If you think something's wrong, then it probably is.*

As I walk out of Dad's office, I put it all to the back of my mind. I haven't even started uni yet and I'm questioning my dad's accounts. He was right this morning. I don't know what I'm talking about.

Something feels weird as I walk towards my bedroom door. It's not shut like I left it, just pulled flush. I live in Dad and Jenny's house, so I guess it's their right to go into their own rooms, but that doesn't stop it feeling like an invasion of privacy. As I push the door open, I realise immediately who's been in here and suddenly I feel uncomfortable for an entirely different reason. Laid out on my bed, in the exact spot I left my ex's black hoodie this morning, is a navy Johnson & Sons one.

I stand frozen, not knowing what to do. I should give it back. Accepting it and wearing it are wrong. It's pushing boundaries that we shouldn't be anywhere near. But it's just a hoodie, right? His actions and words today come back to me, and I fear we might have already blurred a couple of those lines.

In the end, I push my door closed and walk over to the neatly laid-out fabric. In a moment of madness, I swipe it up and bring it to my nose. I'm taken back to the enclosed space of his car when the only thing I was aware of was him sitting next to me. The fullness of his parted lips as he concentrated on where he was going. The gentle rise and fall of his strong chest and the tense muscles as he held onto the steering wheel.

Sitting down on the end of the bed, I try telling myself that the flutters of excitement I feel in my belly are wrong, but it does little to dispel them. In fact, the more I think about our day together, the stronger they get. The need to go and see him nags at me, but I fight it. Putting his hoodie down on my chair, I attempt to distract myself with the TV.

I can only assume that Dad wants to make amends for this morning, because when I venture downstairs a while later for a glass of water, I find him and Jenny in the kitchen, surrounded by food.

"Ah, there you are. We were just going to shout up. Dinner's ready," Jenny sings as if being called down for a family meal is the norm around here.

"I'll go and tell Ben," Dad says, getting up from his stool.

"It's okay, I'll go." I see something flash in Dad's eyes at my suggestion, but when he doesn't say anything, I spin and head back in the direction I came from.

Pausing for a second outside his bedroom door, I suck in a deep breath in preparation for seeing him again. Anticipation engulfs me and I feel like a schoolgirl waiting for her crush to walk into class.

After giving myself a little talking to, I lift my hand and knock. I'm expecting to hear movement from inside, so when I don't, I'm a little disappointed.

"Ben?" I call, and after a few seconds, I push the door handle down. As expected, the room is empty. I guess he's on his usual Saturday night out with his mates. My stomach drops. I stay where I am for a couple of seconds and take in his room. It's tidier than I would have imagined. Stacks of CDs surround his player and a few items of clothing are thrown on a chair, but other than that, it's tidy. The bed's even made.

Closing the door behind me, I make my way back downstairs to embark on what's going to be the most awkward family meal I think I've ever experienced.

BEFORE I GET into bed some time before midnight, I pull the curtains back just to make sure he's not warming the doorstep once again, but there's no sign of him.

I've never really put all that much thought into where he goes and what he does, but suddenly I'm lying here, worrying about him. What if he gets too drunk and one of his friends isn't there to help get him home? What if some other guy starts a fight? All these stupid thoughts run rampant through my head and I end up getting frustrated with myself.

My entire body is tense. Sleep is the last thing on my mind when I eventually hear footsteps creeping up the stairs. My heart races erratically as I picture him getting himself ready for bed.

When I hear a door click much closer than I was expecting, I sit bolt upright in bed. Light filters into my room and I squint as I try to focus on his silhouette in the doorway. My heart pounds in every part of my body as I wait for him to do something.

"Fuck. I shouldn't be here."

I watch, enthralled, as he brings his hands up and scrubs them over his shadowy face.

Expecting him to leave as quickly as he entered, I'm shocked when he reaches out and pushes the door closed. The small amount of light disappears and I'm left with hardly any vision. My other senses are immediately heightened, and the second he steps a foot forward, I stop breathing.

His manly scent gets stronger and goosebumps prick my skin as I wait for what he's going to do.

When he reaches the bed, it dips as he puts his knee on the edge. I'm shocked when he lies down beside me. Reaching for my hand, he encourages me to join him.

We lie with only the sounds of our increased breaths filling the room. My head spins with the knowledge that he's right here, next to me, on my bed.

The pillow rustles as he turns to look at me. I fight to keep my eyes on the darkness in front of me, but eventually the pull to look at him is too strong.

I can just make out his features. His eyes sparkle, reflecting the tiny bit of moonlight seeping in around the curtains.

He searches my face. I've no clue what he's looking for.

I start to think that maybe this is it. That he's come in here just to lie with me and hold my hand. It's not unwelcome. It actually feels pretty incredible, but I'm confused, anxious, and desperate to find out what's really going on in his head.

He rolls onto his side and I follow his lead. The heat from his body burns into me and my fingers twitch to reach out and touch him.

I suck in a breath when his face moves closer to mine. Our eyes stay locked, but, instead of doing what I'm expecting, he rests his forehead against mine. I swear he's trying to tell me something, but my brain's not exactly functioning correctly with him this close to me.

"Fuck," he whispers, nudging his nose against mine. I can almost hear his internal argument. "I can't stop thinking about you," he admits. His honesty forces all the air from my lungs. "Tell me to stop. Tell me to fucking leave. Right now."

I can't. I'm powerless to do anything but lie there and wait. Time seems to stand still as we stare at each other in the darkness.

"Fuck," is the last thing he says before I feel the softness of his lips against mine. His hand lands on my waist, the heat of his palm burning through my top.

He doesn't move to deepen the kiss, but my need for him has my lips parting. The second he feels the movement, he pulls back and stares at me. My eyes have adjusted to the dark enough now to see the tension lining his face.

"Please," I whisper. I can't think of anything worse than him walking out and leaving me alone right now, but it's not enough. No sooner does the word pass my lips, he's up on his feet and backing away from the bed.

"I'm sorry. I shouldn't be here." His voice is full of regret as he stares at me. Eventually, he turns and disappears from my sight. His footsteps thunder down the stairs and the sound of the front door slamming shakes the entire house.

———

BEN NEVER CAME BACK HOME that night, or the next day. Once I knew he'd really left the house that night, I let all my frustration out. I cried for longer than I'm willing to admit. My tears were full of disappointment, regret...and desire. I want to be able to say there was some shame in there, but there wasn't. And in a way, I'm ashamed for not feeling it. Nothing about that kiss and his touch felt shameful. Every moment since he walked out of my room, I've been craving more. More of his kiss. More of his touch. More of everything. He's taking over my thoughts.

It's not until the following Wednesday that I get to lay my eyes on him again since that dark night. I'm sitting, staring at my computer screen, trying to look busy, when the door to the office is pulled open.

I look up. I don't usually bother because no one's ever looking for me, but somehow, my body knows it's him.

Instead of the shirt he should be wearing as he meets with customers, he's clad in a hi-vis jacket and dirty work clothes. Dirt is smeared across both cheeks and his hands are mostly black. Every muscle in my body tenses.

Swallowing, I try to get some moisture back in my mouth and drag my eyes away from him before he notices my attention.

I keep an eye on him over the top of my monitor as he walks in and has a very short and sharp conversation with my dad. I can sense the tension between them from here. I don't miss the tightness of Ben's muscles, the pulsing in his neck, or his clenched fists as he stands just inside the door to the office.

After a few short words, he turns to leave, but at the last minute, he looks up. Our gazes lock and something sparks between us. His eyes brighten but he shows no other signs that he feels the same pull between us that I do.

Our connection only lasts for a couple of seconds, but when he pulls his eyes away and walks out of the office, it's with his shoulders sagging in defeat.

My fingers curl around the base of my chair as I fight my need to follow him, to find out what's going on and why he looks so sad.

"Lauren," Dad barks. "Are you going to answer that or just let it annoy the shit out of all of us?" It's not until Dad's finished talking that I even realise the phone on my desk is ringing. I take a deep breath in an attempt to compose myself before lifting the handset to my ear.

Just like almost every other time it's rung this morning, the caller asks for Jenny or Dad. Most days, I don't feel like I'm needed or really wanted here to do anything with the accounts. Instead, I seem to be becoming Dad's personal PA.

"I'm sorry, but Jenny is out of the office today. I can put you through to Nick." Dad glares at me from his desk. He told me earlier to put off any callers, but after watching the way he was with Ben, I've no real desire to do as I'm told.

Thankfully, after he's taken the phone call he didn't want, Dad leaves the office. The atmosphere immediately lightens and Erica even puts the radio on, which is banned while the boss is around.

The day goes on forever, my thoughts consumed by the look on Ben's face as he dragged his gaze away from me earlier. Every time I hear the main door to the office squeak, my heart jumps into my throat, but he never reappears. I can only hope he might make it home tonight so at least I can find out if he's okay.

"We're going out tonight," Erica announces after following me into the kitchen to get her lunch from the fridge.

"Tonight?"

"Yeah. Wednesday's the new Friday."

"I thought every night was a Friday night in London," I grin.

"Exactly." She winks at me, throwing her tub of leftovers into the microwave. "You've been moping for days. You need a good blow out. I'll shoot a message out to the guys. They'll be on board."

I know it's pointless arguing, but to be honest, a night out and letting loose does sound like a good idea. I almost ask her not to tell the guys because the last thing I need is Ben ruining another night for me, but I bite the words back, knowing it'll only invite unwanted questions.

"Yeah, okay."

"I'm going to have to work a little late, though. How about you go home and grab your stuff, then we'll get ready together at mine? I've already got tequila in the fridge."

"Sounds good."

The more I think about it as the afternoon wears on, the more I'm looking forward to it. Erica keeps me informed about who's coming, and when I don't hear that Ben's presence is confirmed, I feel even better about it. The last thing I need is him trying to ruin my evening by telling me what I should and shouldn't be doing.

"Girl! You look hot," Erica sings when I step into

the kitchen in the house she shares with her sister. She runs her eyes up and down my body, nodding in approval. I'm wearing a black leather skirt and a gold sequined cami with an open back. "I'm going to have to pry the men off you tonight."

"What if I don't want you to?" I ask with a wink.

"Ooh, are you planning on hooking up?"

I make a non-committal noise because I'm fully aware that I'm not hooking up with some random guy in a club, but Erica doesn't need to know that. It seems to be what she does every weekend, so I may as well look like I fit in. I also have no intention of mentioning that I'm still a virgin.

"Here, drink this. My sister's going to drop us off in a minute."

With the tequila flowing through my system, I manage to put everything with Ben to one side and just enjoy myself. We meet some of the guys, but thankfully both Will and Ben are noticeably absent. I try not to look too relieved about it.

After a round of drinks, we head out onto the dance floor. Erica and I dance with James and Stewart, two of the builders from work. The four of us let loose, not worrying about what we look like or who's watching us making fools of ourselves. The dancing is mostly innocent, but there's the occasional bump and grind when the song commands it.

Leaning into Erica, I shout in her ear that I'm heading to the toilet and she waves me off. Weaving my way through the packed dance floor, I eventually make it to the to the other side of the room to where I need to be.

After fighting with the women trying to touch up their make-up in the mirrors, it seems like forever when I eventually make it out again.

I'm about to walk down the corridor to re-join the main room when someone wraps their hand around my wrist. I fight to free myself, simultaneously turning to see who it is. My breath catches and the fight leaves me as I stare into the blue eyes of my stepbrother.

His stare holds mine for a beat before he pulls me towards the stairs. We go down one flight and then he continues moving towards the dance floor. The music's different on this level—the bass is louder, the tempo sexy and seductive.

As he drags me in front of him, his hands land on my waist and he pulls me back against his body. A loud sigh leaves me when our bodies align and I feel him move against me.

His fingers tickle at my shoulder as he moves my hair, exposing my skin. Dropping his head, his nose runs up the length of my neck before I feel his lips at my ear.

"I couldn't watch you dancing with someone else any longer," he growls, pulling us even closer. I gasp when I feel his length against my arse.

He grinds his hips with mine, keeping perfect time with the song booming through the speakers, but I barely hear any of it. My focus is solely on the connection of our bodies.

His lips trail down my neck, his tongue sneaking out to taste my skin, and something inside me explodes. Heat blooms between my legs and the only thing I want is to be in a room alone with him, not in a club full of sweaty strangers.

"Jesus fucking Christ, Lauren. I shouldn't need you this much."

Turning in his arms, I look up at him. His pupils are dilated and his lips parted, his chest heaving. His tongue runs across the bottom lip and I'm just about to close the distance between us when he looks up.

His eyes widen before he lets me go and disappears into the crowd. My body aches for him the second he leaves.

"There you are," Erica shouts, walking up to me and immediately breaking out some moves like the most erotic moment of my life didn't just happen where we're standing. "Are you okay?"

"Yeah. Sorry, I bumped into someone I knew."

"That's okay. Just let me know next time you want to disappear, yeah?"

"Sure. I...uh...actually, I think I'm going to head home."

"What? It's still early."

"I know, but I'm wiped. I'll see you in the morning?"

"Sure. Text me when you get home."

Waving, I get the hell out of that club as fast as I can. Every single part of me is desperate to hunt through the entire place to find Ben. Just how badly I need him is enough to make me go home. Nothing good can come of the strength of my feelings.

Thanks to my long day and night, I crash the second my head hits my pillow. That doesn't mean my dreams aren't full of *him* and how differently the night could have ended if we weren't interrupted.

WHEN I WAKE the next morning, I'm feeling much fresher than I deserve to be after a night out. I can't say the same for Erica when she shows up to work almost an hour late. She looks like she's just fallen straight out the club...or maybe some guy's bed. The day's crazy and the phone doesn't stop ringing, so I don't get the opportunity to hear about the rest of her night. From the look of the love bite on her neck, I'm pretty sure I don't want the details, anyway.

I'm becoming used to the silence, and it's no different when I let myself into the house after work that evening. Jenny's car is in the driveway, but there's no sign of her once again.

After making myself a drink, I head up to my room to change into something more comfortable. I decide to have a shower and wash my hair because the one I had this morning was way too quick to properly wash last night off me. I strip out of my work clothes and step under the hot spray.

I stand there for the longest time with my head tipped forward, allowing the powerful jets of water to massage my tense shoulders. I knew moving here and living with Dad wasn't going to be a walk in the park, but I never imagined it would be quite like this.

I've no idea how much time's passed when I eventually stand in front of the mirror and remove what's left of today's make-up. My usually light blue eyes seem to have much more grey in them as I stare at myself. I might be trying to put Ben and this thing between us to the back of my mind, but I'd be kidding myself if I thought I was being successful.

I'm lost in my own head as I walk from the ensuite wrapped in only a towel. I'm not expecting to have company, so a little squeal passes my lips when I find Ben sat on the edge of my bed, waiting for me. His hair's still damp from his own shower and he's wearing a dark pair of slim-fit jeans with a white t-shirt that looks like it's been painted on his skin.

I freeze just inside the room and my stomach knots. His eyes widen and I watch them darken as he runs them leisurely around my almost bare, and still slightly wet, body.

"Well, my day's sure looking up."

Pulling the towel around me tighter, I walk over to my dresser.

"What's up?"

"Plenty," he says after clearing his throat. "I just wanted to make sure you were okay."

"Yeah, I'm good. Why?" I can only assume he's asking about what happened last night.

"No reason." He's lying. I can see it in his eyes. "You hungry?"

"I am."

"Have dinner with me?"

"Uh...sure. Can you cook?"

"I wasn't thinking of that kind of dinner." I swear I see a little colour rise to his cheeks, but I must be mistaken because there's no way the brooding, cocky man stood in front of me gets embarrassed. Ever.

"You mean, go out?" *Like a date?* I want to ask,

but I manage to keep the question in. I could be interpreting this so incredibly wrong, which would mean asking my stepbrother if he wants to take me out on a date is a very bad idea.

"Yeah. As much as I hate to suggest it, get dressed and we'll go." His eyes run the length of me once again and tingles follow their movement around my body. Biting down on my bottom lip, I refrain from suggesting getting takeout and not leaving this room. There's no way I should be having these thoughts, and he definitely shouldn't be looking at me like he is right now.

I start to think he's not going to leave, but after another lap around my body, he gets himself up and walks to the door. "I'll wait in the car," he says over his shoulder before pulling it closed behind him.

"WHAT WAS wrong with waiting in the house?" I ask when I fall down onto his passenger seat a little over thirty minutes later. I tried to be as fast as I could, but there was no way I was going out with him looking like he does, and me with wet hair and no make-up.

"You've probably noticed that it isn't my favourite place to be," he says, casting a glance towards the mini-mansion we both call home before looking over at me. "And your dad's d—Whoa." His lips curl up in sexy smile and his eyes darken as he takes me in.

I had no idea where we were going, and I wasn't given a lot of time to make a decision about what to wear. In the end, I slid my favourite white skirt up my legs, teamed it with a black and white striped vest and a pair of wedges. My blonde hair is loosely hanging around my shoulders and my make-up is light. I thought I looked okay when I gave myself a once-over in the mirror before I left the room, but seeing the look on Ben's face makes me feel like a million dollars.

"You look..." He trails off and I watch the muscles in his neck ripple as he swallows. "Incredible."

"Thank you," I whisper, suddenly feeling nervous about our impending evening together. When his eyes come back up to mine, something sparks between us and my skin tingles with awareness.

"I shouldn't be doing this," he says, but it seems to be more to himself than me.

"We're just going for dinner."

His dark stare turns my way, and a shiver runs

down my spine. "Just dinner," he repeats. "But what about all the other things I want to do?"

My mouth waters as thoughts of what he could be suggesting run through my head.

"Shit." His sudden outburst has me flinching before I reach for the seatbelt and strap myself in as Ben slams his foot to the floor and speeds away from the house.

"What the hell was that?" I ask, seeing Dad's car turn into the driveway after us.

"It's probably best he doesn't see us together."

"What? Why?"

"You're his little girl, Lauren. He wants to protect you."

"I don't need protecting from you."

"You sure about that?"

CHAPTER FIVE

SOMETHING CHANGED with Ben after he saw my dad. He shut himself down like he's too scared to show me who he really is. I hate the idea that I could have given him any indication that he can't be himself with me.

The pub he brought me to is one I've not been to before. It looks like an old London boozer from the outside, but inside it's modern and bright, and the food is out of this world. It's nowhere near what I pictured when Ben mentioned dinner. I may have decided against suggesting it was a date, but that's very much what it feels like—aside from his weirdness where our parents are concerned.

"I guess we should get back," I say regretfully once he's insisted on paying the bill.

"Do we have to?"

"Why do you hate it so much?"

"You like living there?"

"Uh..." I try to come up with something diplomatic, but my silence must say it all.

"Exactly."

"Why don't you move out? You must earn good money from the business. You don't need to stay."

"I have my reasons." Raising my eyebrows, I wait for him to continue. "Not today," he says, standing from his chair and holding his hand out for me.

Sparks shoot up my arm the second our skin connects, and his eyes flash to mine. He felt it, too.

Together, we walk out of the pub and towards his car. "Do you mind if we just drive for a bit? I'm not ready for this to end yet."

"Of course." The sadness in his voice ensures I'll do whatever he wants. "You know you can tell me anything, right?"

"Trust me when I tell you that you don't want to know."

"But—"

"Lauren, please. Don't."

"Okay, okay. But I'm here, if you need me." Reaching my hand out, I hesitate a few inches from him. Sensing what I'm going to do, he threads our fingers together and places our joined hands on his lap.

He blows out a long breath, and when he glances over at me, I see some of his earlier tension has vanished. It's as if looking into my eyes calms him somehow.

"Thank you," he whispers before turning back to the road.

"For what?"

"This. Everything. For just being here."

I lose track of the direction we go in, and it's not long until I've no clue where we are. Ben seems to know, though, and eventually he pulls the car to a stop in a deserted car park.

"Wow," I breathe, taking in the bright lights of the city in the distance.

"I spend a lot of time here."

"And there I was, thinking you were out getting drunk every night."

"Oh, I do that, too," he chuckles.

It warms me from the inside out, knowing that I can make him laugh. It's not something he seems to do very often, and it only makes me want to make him do it more. His bad boy image lessens when he laughs and he looks more his age. "I've never brought anyone here before." His voice suddenly takes on a more sombre tone.

"Thank you for sharing it with me."

Dropping his hands from the wheel, he reaches over and once again entwines our fingers.

"Things haven't been easy for me in that house, Lauren. I won't taint you with the details, but it was my dad's dream home. He and my granddad build it with their bare hands. Every day, it's a reminder of everything I've lost."

"I'm so sorry." Bringing his hand up, I press my lips against his rough knuckles.

"I know I'm not the easiest person to get on with or even to share a house with, but Mum needs me."

I want to tell him that she's not his responsibility, that she's got my dad to do that now, but I know it's not what he needs to hear. And I've spent years keeping an eye out for my mum, so I do understand what he's saying. "What about what you need? Who supports you?"

He shrugs. My heart breaks for him. I've heard stories about how close he was to both his dad and granddad. I can only imagine how their deaths have affected him.

His phone vibrating in his pocket ends our little moment. He lets go of my hand to slide his phone out. Groaning when he looks at the illuminated screen, he cancels the call and throws it down into one of the cup holders between us.

"So…what do you want to do now?" I ask when a tense silence descends around us.

"You want the truth?" Turning his head, he stares at me. The darkness in his eyes is almost a warning and my stomach turns over, although I'm pretty sure it's only excitement I'm feeling.

"Always," I whisper eventually.

Reaching over, he takes my cheek in his warm hand and leans forward. I find myself doing the same and, in seconds, our lips are almost touching.

"I shouldn't have done that the other night. It was wrong—"

"But…" I say, sensing there's more.

"I can't stop thinking about it. About you."

"Me, either," I admit quietly.

"Fuck, Lauren. We shouldn't be doing this."

"Says who? As far as I can tell, the only two people who matter are—" My words are cut off when he closes the tiny amount of space between us. His lips part and his tongue finds its way in. His taste explodes in my mouth, my tongue running along his, eager to explore.

His hand cups my other cheek and he tilts my head to the side with his fingers in my hair to deepen the kiss.

I've been kissed a couple of times in the past, but never like this. It's intense. Explosive. Consuming.

Everything I previously had in my head vanishes, and the only thing on my mind is getting more of Ben.

Reaching out, I place my hands on his solid chest. I need to feel him. I need more than his lips. Every inch of my body aches for him, for his touch. So, when his hands slide down to my waist and he lifts me, I eagerly help to climb over the centre console until I'm sitting across his lap.

With his large hands around my waist, I settle myself into the kiss, but it's not long before even feeling him beneath me isn't enough. My head might not know what I should be doing in this situation, but it seems that my body is fully on board.

Needing more, I lift the hem of his t-shirt and go to run my hands up the taut skin of his stomach. But the second our skin connects, he rips his lips from mine.

"Shit. Fuck, Lauren. What the hell are we doing?" he pants, his eyes wide and his lips swollen.

Pressing his forehead to mine, his breath tickles across my face as I try to get control of my breathing. With his hands still on me and his solid thighs between my legs, it's not all that easy.

Ben's phone vibrates in the cup holder once again. After letting out a long breath, he breaks the connection between us and lifts me back into the passenger seat.

"I'm sor—"

"Don't," I snap.

"Let's go home." The sadness in his voice has me almost jumping back onto his lap. My fingers grip the leather beneath me to make me stay put as Ben starts the car.

Before putting it into reverse, he looks over at me. I open my mouth to say something, anything to take the pained look from his face, but he beats me to it.

"This is for the best." I'm not sure who he's trying to convince because I'm pretty sure neither of us truly believes that.

I never would have thought it, but the brooding boy who's avoided me at all costs in the past makes me feel alive in a way I never have before. I know he's trying to do the right thing, but damn if the only thing I want to do right now is break all the rules.

There's no way we should be doing this. No one, other than us, will understand this pull, this incredible connection. The thought makes my heart drop. I could have found the one person most people spend most of their lives looking for...and he's the one person I never should have looked twice at.

"ARE YOU READY?" Ben asks after we've sat in the driveway in darkness and silence for a few minutes.

I desperately want to say no, that I'm not ready for our time together to be over, but he doesn't need to hear it. His entire body is tense. I know he's struggling with this just as much as I am.

"Maybe we should run away." I suggest it as a joke, but when he turns to look at me, his eyes are deadly serious.

"Do not tempt me, Lauren," he warns. The deepness of his voice hits me and I swallow a ball of emotion that threatens to form in my throat. He really hates it here. I wish he'd open up. I just want to understand, to help in any way I can.

"Come on, let's get this over with."

I don't understand the concern in his tone. All we're doing is going home. What's he got to be so concerned about?

Everything starts to make a little more sense the second the front door clicks shut. Suddenly, all Ben's ignored phone calls and his worry about coming back make sense.

"Get in here right now," Dad booms from the living room.

Dread fills me. Looking over at Ben, his lips are pressed into a thin line, his eyes hard and angry.

I squeeze his forearm and make him look down at me. "It's okay. I've got this."

"I'm not leaving you with him."

Ben doesn't get to say any more because Dad staggers into the doorway, leaning against the frame for support. He's drunk.

"What the fuck do you think you're doing?" he hollers, his angry eyes focused on Ben. I immediately drop my arm and step in front of him. He shouldn't have to deal with Dad like this.

Dad's eyes don't move from Ben, even with me trying to distract him.

"Go upstairs, Lauren," Ben says behind me.

"No."

"Lauren," Ben growls. "You don't need to be in the middle of this."

"But—"

"Do as you're fucking told for once, kid," Dad barks. Tears sting my eyes at his belittling tone. With a quick glance at Ben, I run from the room and up the stairs.

"Shut your door and put some music on," Ben says when my foot hits the first step, but I don't respond.

My heart pounds and my hands tremble as I sit on the top step and wait for the shouting to start.

I'm not disappointed, and suddenly I understand

why Ben hates it here so much. My dad really doesn't like him. I just don't understand why. So what if he's a little moody and comes in late, drunk? He's a twenty-year-old guy—that's fairly normal. It's probably no different to what he did at that age.

I can't make out all of Dad's words from up here. He's too drunk and most are so slurred that I doubt even Ben has a clue what he's saying. But I hear his warning loud and clear. "I told you to stay the hell away from her. If I find out you've so much as laid a finger on her, I'll fucking kill you."

My stomach knots. I've never heard my dad talk like that before. Never heard him so vicious. I've hidden myself away from plenty of arguments between him and Mum in the past, even him and Jenny on a very rare occasion, but he's never threatened either of them like that.

The second I hear footsteps, I jump up and run to my room, not wanting either of them to know I was listening.

Sitting on the end of my bed, I try to figure out what I'm going to say to Dad when he's sobered up. There's no way that Ben and I won't be spending any more time together. The connection between us will make that physically impossible, especially when he sleeps just across the hallway.

CHAPTER SIX

MY MIND RACES and my heart pounds as I wait to hear Ben come home. Dad crashed his way up to bed not so long ago; he's probably passed out by now, so I know the coast is clear.

Grabbing my phone, I quickly type him a message.

> Lauren: Come back. Please. It's safe.

I stare at the screen for ages, but it never shows that the message has been read and I get no response.

Breathing out a frustrated sigh, I turn over once again, trying to figure out what the hell my dad's issue with him is. As far as I'm concerned, Ben's done nothing wrong since the day they were first introduced, but then I'm always kept in the dark.

Even living here, I feel like everything important is discussed when I'm out of earshot. It's frustrating as hell.

I've almost given up hope that he's going to reappear when I hear his footsteps creaking on the stairs. Holding my breath, I wait, hoping he'll come to me like he did last time. But when a door clicks open, it's not mine.

I force myself to wait a whole minute before throwing my legs over the side of the bed and getting up.

I knock on his door just to be polite, because what I really want to do is storm in and demand some answers.

When he doesn't answer, I push the handle down and invite myself in. The second my eyes land on him, I panic. He's too focused on filling a bag full of his stuff to notice my arrival. My heart picks up pace at the thought of him leaving.

Wasting no time, I race over and place my hand on his forearm. He flinches before dragging his eyes over to me. He looks exhausted, the deep frown line between his brows showing how much of a toll my dad's putting on his life.

"Ben, I—"

"I can't do this, Lauren. Just walk back out and pretend you didn't see this."

The sadness in his voice guts me.

"No. No way. I won't let him push you away like this. This is your home. It's where you belong. Your business is where you belong."

He casts his eyes over my shoulder, his expression dropping even more, if that's possible. "This isn't my home. It's just a place I stay to try to protect those I love. The business hasn't been mine in a long time. It never will be. It's time I accepted my life for what it is and try to do something about it."

"No, please," I beg, ducking under his arm that's still holding on to the bag on his bed. I slide up his body, and the spark that I'm becoming to expect when we're together crackles between us. "You're better than just running from this. You've got more here than you think. Can't you feel that?" I ask, my heart pounding with fear that I'm the only one with these crazy feelings.

His eyes flash with awareness and an acceptance that, even if he opens his mouth and denies it, I know he'd be lying.

"I can't, Lauren. You deserve so much better than what I can offer you."

"Bullshit," I bark. "Do not believe any of the crap my dad tells you. You are so much more than he thinks. Don't run from him. Prove who you are."

"Don't you think I've tried? I have, time and time

again. I've done everything I thought was expected of me, but still...he's taken everything and turned everyone against me."

"No one's against you." I think of Jenny and everyone at work. Sure, they don't all sing about how wonderful he is, but they certainly like him well enough.

"You so sure about that?"

"Yeah, and my dad...he's just being protective."

Anger fills his eyes. "I told you to shut yourself in your room tonight."

"I don't always do what I'm told, Ben. It's time people started learning that I'm an adult who can make my own decisions. As soon as Dad's sobered up, I'm going to talk to him about tonight. I'm—"

"Don't even think about it. You coming to my defence isn't going to help my case."

"But—"

"There are no buts here, Lauren. He won't accept this." His eyes drop to where we're still pressed up against one another. "He'll never accept this."

"So, who gives a fuck what he thinks? Who made him God?"

"Lauren," he warns, but I can already tell I've won. The anger that was in his eyes has been replaced by something else entirely.

Lust.

His gaze stays on mine for a few more seconds before dropping to my lips. I wet them in preparation and I've barely got my tongue back in my mouth before he's on me. His lips press against mine and his tongue sweeps into my mouth. His hands slide up my waist and around my back, holding me tight and bringing us even closer together. My curves mould against his hard, muscular body and I melt under his touch.

Groaning into his kiss, I find the bottom of his t-shirt and run my fingers up the warm, smooth skin of his back. When I start to drag my nails down, he moans and starts to harden against my stomach.

Excitement flutters in my belly that I have this power over him. He's the bad boy that every woman I know lusts after. All my friends want him and the women at work wish they had the chance. But I'm here, in his arms, with his lips pressed against mine.

All the reasons why this really shouldn't be happening are far from my mind as I lose myself to his touch. My skin burns wherever he touches me, and my body aches for more.

Shifting his hands to my thighs, he grips and lifts me so I have no choice but to wrap my legs around his waist. His hardness presses against me. A wave of sensations I've not experienced before explode from my centre. Pulling my lips from his, I suck in a surprised breath. His hooded eyes lock on mine as he rolls his hips. The same thing happens again, only it's stronger this time. A sexy and determined smirk tugs at his lips, making something unfurl inside of me.

"Ben, please." I've no idea what I'm asking for, but whatever it is, I need it. I need it badly.

Dropping his lips to my neck, he kisses the sensitive skin below my ear. Goosebumps spread across my body and heat plumes in my belly.

Holy shit, I want him is the only thing I can think as he lowers me to the bed.

But instead of continuing, he stands and goes to walk away.

"What are you doing? Come back." My words come out in a rush. My need for him has heat hitting my cheeks and spreading down my neck.

"Patience," he says with a chuckle.

The second he flips the lock on his bedroom door, something heavy settles in my lower stomach. *Oh my God, this is happening.* I probably should be scared, but that's the last thing I'm feeling as I watch Ben cross the room, scroll through his phone, and then turn on his speaker. Before turning back to me, he reaches behind him and drags his t-shirt over his head.

"Holy cow," I whisper, more to myself than him,

when he turns towards me. Not only are his eyes so dark they're almost black, but what I always knew to be a muscular body is so much more than I ever imagined. I didn't think bodies like that existed in real life. The dark tattoo I didn't know he had wraps around his ribs, a stark contrast to his lightly tanned skin.

"You know it's rude to stare." Amusement fills his voice as he slowly stalks back over to me, his eyes never leaving mine.

"S—sorry, I just..." I stutter, not really sure what I should be saying in this situation.

"I'm joking, Lauren. I don't want anyone else's eyes on me but yours."

I'm not stupid. I know he's been with plenty of women. I've even had the pleasure of bumping into a few after he's kicked them out. But it's easy to put all of that to one side when he's looking at me with longing in his eyes like he is right now.

"I shouldn't be doing this. I think we both know I don't have the right to take anything from you."

"I'll give you everything you want. I'm yours."

The muscles in his neck and shoulders tense, but his lips stay pressed into a hard line.

"You're not mine to take. But I can make you feel so fucking good." With those words, he wraps his fingers around the waistband of my shorts and drags them and my knickers down my legs.

I gasp, embarrassment filling me momentarily, but no sooner has he dropped them to the floor, he sits me up and pulls my lips to his. His kiss washes away any concern and embarrassment I have. And by the time he's kissing down my neck and curling his fingers around the bottom of the hoodie he gave me, I'm panting for more.

The sweatshirt joins the rest of my discarded clothes before he peels my vest from me. My breasts feel heavy, my nipples peaked painfully, and it only gets worse when his eyes drop to take them in.

"You're so fucking beautiful. Too fucking pure and innocent for the likes of me."

Pushing me back to the bed, he kisses across my collarbone and then down over the swell of one breast.

I'm not totally innocent. I've done things with guys in the past, but each encounter was a rush job just to get them off. I've never experienced anything like this—being adored and worshipped. Having my own pleasure matter.

My back arches as he sucks one of my sensitive nipples into his mouth.

"Oh God, Ben."

He looks up at me and another pool of lust explodes between my legs.

"Oh, please...oh...oh," I chant as he kisses lower.

The music in the background barely registers in my head, but as I continue whimpering, I understand why he put it on. This house might be massive, with our parents' bedroom at the other end of the L-shaped corridor, but neither of us needs to risk being heard. I tell myself to keep it together and get control of my volume, but the second I feel his tongue gently lick at me, I cry out in pleasure.

I fist the sheets beneath me when he adds a little more pressure before sliding a finger inside me. I've no idea if the words and cries falling from my lips are intelligible or not, but I don't really care. What he's doing has taken over ever inch of my body, and I never want him to stop.

My body coils tighter and tighter and I know that, at some point, something's got to give. When I feel him slide another finger into me, that something inside me snaps.

White light flashes behind my eyes as my entire body explodes with a sensation beyond anything I've felt before. I feel it in the tips of my fingers and all the way to my toes.

It feels like it lasts forever, but as I come down from my high and lock eyes with Ben, who's still between my thighs, I realise it wasn't nearly long enough.

There's pride in his eyes, but the overwhelming emotion is sadness. My initial thought is that I'm about to be sent on my way when all I really want is more of him.

When he sits up, I'm just about prepared for what's to come. Without words, I know that's as far as he's going to take this.

I prop myself up, ready to do the walk of shame back to my room, but, to my surprise, he doesn't say anything. Instead, he stands, drops his jeans to the floor, and pulls the covers back beside me. Sliding under, he looks at me with anticipation. There's a vulnerability oozing from him, something I'm sure he doesn't allow many people to see.

Jumping into action, I lift my arse and climb under the covers with him. The second I stretch my body out, he rolls onto his side and pulls me to him.

"Why did you—"

"Shh...I won't take any more from you than that. It's not my place," he says, repeating his earlier words.

"But I said—"

"That doesn't matter. I need to do what's right. Well...some of it, at least." A sad laugh passes his lips.

"Please, let me in." I press my hand to his chest,

feeling the steady beat of his heart beneath. "Please, I could help make things better."

"It'll only make life harder for you. Promise me you won't say anything to your dad. Don't try to fight for me." The look on his face has me agreeing, even though it's the last thing I want to do.

I fall asleep in his arms.

When I wake the next morning, he's gone.

CHAPTER SEVEN

THE MOMENT I realise I'm alone, I pick up my discarded clothes and run back to my room. I can still smell him on me and the last thing I want to do is wash it away, but I know I have to put last night behind me. I have a nagging feeling that last night was the beginning and the end of anything between us. The most sensible thing to do would be to put it behind me and try to move on.

"Lauren, is that you?" Dad asks the second I step foot downstairs.

"Yeah," I call as I make my way towards the kitchen.

"I'm sorry if I was angry last night. It's just that Ben isn't someone I think you should be spending time with." The vicious tone has gone, replaced by one that sounds a little like regret. "He's bad news.

You've got plenty of other friends I'm sure you'd enjoy being with much more."

"He's not bad news, Dad. I think you've got him all wrong." Something darkens in his eyes, but it's gone again in a flash.

"Just trust me on this, okay?"

Ben's words from last night about not fighting for him come back to me. As much as I want to do just that, I trust him more than I do my dad right now, so I swallow the words on the tip of my tongue and instead whisper my agreement.

"Jenny and I are going away this weekend. I suggest you go and stay with your mother."

"Dad, I'm more than capable of staying here without you."

"This isn't up for discussion, Lauren. Don't you want to spend time with your mother?"

"Of course I do, but you can't just move me in and out when it suits you," I mutter.

"It's my house, young lady," he snaps, and I see a little of the person he was last night seeping in.

"No, Dad. It's Jenny's house. I'm nineteen in a few weeks. I'm more than capable of being home alone and not burning the place to the ground."

"*That* isn't what I'm concerned about."

"Oh, and what is it exactly that you're concerned about?" Raising an eyebrow, I wait for his response.

The silence stretches out between us before the noise of my phone going off sounds out like a siren. Ignoring it, I continue to stare at my dad.

"Give the girl a break, Nick. She's more than welcome to stay here while we're away," Jenny says, joining us out of nowhere.

Dad turns his stare on her, giving me a chance to look at my phone.

> Ben: You are NOT going to your mum's this weekend.

Looking up, I glance around for him. My body is aware that he's looking at me, but I don't see him. That is, until a shadow catches my eye when it moves from the top of the stairs. He may not have been in bed when I woke this morning, but he's keeping a close eye on me—protecting me, just like he said he intended to do.

Once I know he's gone, I look back down at my message and butterflies take flight in my stomach at the prospect of an entire weekend alone with him.

"You'd better be texting your mother," my dad grumbles, having finished his debate with Jenny, "Because if you don't arrange it, I will."

"Yeah, of course."

"I'll be checking," he warns, earning himself another look of disappointment from Jenny.

I want to argue with him, but the knowledge that everything he seems to be scared of happening probably will happen once the two of us are alone has the words dying on my tongue.

A whole weekend with Ben in an empty house. Some of the sensations he created in my body last night tingle within me, making me desperate for the weekend.

***

I DON'T GET a chance to make a plan to fool Dad into believing I'm with Mum this weekend, because the second I get to work, things go crazy. It's probably not helped by the fact that I've only had a few hours' sleep, and when I do get a quiet moment, my thoughts immediately transport me back to Ben's bed and how it felt to have his hands and lips on me.

I squirm in my seat once again and my face flames red when it doesn't go unnoticed by Erica.

"You okay, Lauren? You should book a doctor's appointment for that." She winks.

My cheeks have barely cooled down when my skin tingles and a shiver runs down my spine.

He's here.

It's only another two seconds before the door opens and Ben marches into the office. I look up, desperate to see him after everything that happened between us, but he doesn't even look my way.

Disappointment fills me.

I watch as he walks straight up to Laura at the other end of the office and starts asking about some delivery and hiring some lifters for the job he's working on.

The whole time I sit there, unable to take my eyes off him, willing him to look my way so that I know I didn't imagine what was between us. If the pull I feel is really there, surely he's fighting not to look my way right now.

As their conversation comes to an end, my heart starts to race. Surely now he'll acknowledge my presence?

Instead, he turns towards my dad's office, lets out a long breath and walks in—without knocking like everyone else does, of course.

With my frustration growing by the minute, I push my chair out behind me and mutter something about going to make tea before disappearing into our little kitchen and flicking the kettle on.

It takes forever to boil. Or, at least it feels that way as I fight to keep thoughts of him being in the other room from my mind. Being able to hear his deep rumbling voice through the thin wall doesn't help all that much.

I turn to start filling a mug when I sense someone join me. His unique scent mixed with hard work hits my nose. Lust rolls through me.

His heat warms my back before his hot lips land on my bare neck.

I moan as he tickles across my sensitive skin. "I missed you this morning."

"Sorry, I needed...a run," he stutters, like he isn't really telling the truth.

Movement from the office has him jumping back. His hand slides into mine and he pulls me into the ladies' toilets.

Once in the cubicle, he pins me back against the door with his hips. His lips land on mine and he gives me what I've been craving since waking up alone.

Him.

As the kiss deepens, my need for him grows and so does his length against my stomach. I'm fully aware that he must have fallen asleep with the bluest balls known to man last night. It's something I'm keen to fix as soon as possible.

Slipping my hand down between us, I stroke him over the fabric of his trousers. The growl that rumbles up his throat only encourages me and I begin fiddling with the button so I can gain access, until his large hand wraps around my forearm and stops my movement.

"Lauren, not here." His voice is pained. Stopping is the last thing he wants right now.

But it's the sensible thing to do. We need to be careful. If last night and this morning with Dad taught me anything, it's that we cannot be caught. I've no idea what this thing is between us, but for now, whatever it is needs to be kept secret.

He steps back from me and I miss him the second our bodies part. It's crazy because he's stood right in front of me, but it's like my body needs his to be whole.

I take him in as he stands there with his chest heaving, his eyes dark and full of lust, his cock trying to break through his trousers.

I can't help but bite down on my bottom lip as I stare. Fuck, I want to see him with every piece of clothing gone. I want to give him the same treatment he gave me last night. I want to make him feel so damn good. My mouth waters at the thought of having him inside me. It's probably a good thing that he starts talking, distracting me from my sinful thoughts.

"Tell me you'll sort out this weekend. This might be the only chance we get to be properly alone for a long time."

"It'll be fine. I'll just tell Dad I've spoken to Mum and I'm staying there."

"He'll check, Lauren. I'd put money on it. You need to get your mum on side. Tell her whatever, but you need her to back you up."

What we're doing suddenly seems so real, and I panic. How are we going to keep this from Dad when it's happening under his roof? And even worse, what will happen when he finds out? I've no doubt he will, at some point.

"I will."

Excitement fills his eyes before he moves towards me once again and steals another knee-weakening kiss.

"Don't be surprised if you don't see me until they've gone. It's not because I don't want to be with you, I just don't want to raise any kind of suspicion," he whispers against my lips.

My stomach drops and suddenly tomorrow night feels like it's years away. "Okay."

"Hey," he says, tipping my chin up so I have no choice but to look at him. "There's no other way I want to spend my time than with you, but we need to be careful. One day, Lauren. One day, what we do will be up to us, but now's not that time. Tomorrow night can't come soon enough, and I promise to give you the best weekend of your life."

I nod against him and, with one last kiss, he slips out of the cubicle and he's gone. Gone until tomorrow night when all we have is each other. My stomach flutters with excitement.

When I walk back to finish the job I started, I find Erica stood in my place, filling the mugs. "I thought we were all going to die of dehydration," she says with a laugh when she sees me coming.

"Sorry, I...uh..."

"Got distracted?" she asks with a knowing smirk. My face must show my panic. "Hey, it's okay. Your secret's safe with me. I must warn you, though, it's not going to go down well with everyone." She casts a quick look over her shoulder to where my dad's office sits on the other side of the wall.

My lip trembles as everything that's happened in the past few weeks with Ben hits me all at once.

"Hey now," Erica shushes, pulling me in for a hug. I focus on my breathing to prevent myself from breaking down in her arms. Turning into an emotional wreck at work is the last thing I need right now. "Why don't you get out of here for the day? Go and treat yourself to something nice. I'll tell your dad you weren't feeling well."

"You don't need to do that." Pulling back from her, I look up into her kind eyes. Erica might only be two years older than me, but she's figured Dad out and somehow manages to get exactly what she wants.

"We're only young once, Lauren. And if I

eavesdropped correctly, your dad and Jenny are out of town this weekend, right? You probably need time to get prepared," she says with a cheeky wink.

I can't help the laugh that falls from my lips before a more serious thought fills my mind. "You don't think..." I trail off, not knowing if I really want someone else's opinion on what I'm about to ask.

"I don't think what?"

"That it's...*wrong*?" I whisper, feeling a little ashamed for the first time.

"Lauren," she breathes. "The only thing stopping you is your own mind. People might frown upon it, but the reality is that you're not blood related. It's not illegal or whatever. None of us can help who we fall for. If he treats you right and makes you feel like a better version of yourself, then who is anyone to stop you? Plus, there's also his killer good looks and god-like body, so how were you ever going to say no?"

I know words are just that, *her* words, but they make me feel a hell of a lot better. "I knew there was something. The way he looks at you. I'd pay for a man to look at me with that kind of passion in his eyes. Now, get out of here. Go!"

Grabbing my stuff, I rush out of the office before anyone else spots me. I walk down to the tube station, intending to head home, but when I get to the bottom of the escalator, I turn left instead of right, deciding at the last minute to take Erica's advice and spend the afternoon getting prepared for the weekend.

***

WITH FRESHLY COLOURED hair and arms full of bags, I put the key in the door and step inside.

"Lauren, oh my God. I've missed you!" Mum calls the second she hears my arrival. "Wow, look at you." After taking in my new hair, she grabs my shoulders and pulls me into a tight hug. We talk most days, but being in her arms again has tears stinging my eyes.

"I hope you haven't eaten. I brought our favourite," I say, holding up a bag of Thai takeout.

"No, I haven't. Come on, I want to hear everything."

Following Mum down to our little kitchen, I sit myself at the table while she dishes up and makes us both a drink. All the while, I go over and over what I'm going to say to her to get her on board for this weekend. I've always told Mum everything, and I think the only way I'm going to get away with this is to be honest. Even if I have no idea what she's going to think.

"So..." she asks, once she's settled opposite me. "What's it really like living in the show home?"

"Pretty much what I expected. There's hardly ever anyone home, and when they are, they're not exactly what I consider welcoming and friendly. Other than the quick commute to work, I'm still wondering why you thought it was such a good idea." I quirk an eyebrow at her, hoping she'll give me more.

"It's good to get out of your comfort zone every now and then, Lauren. I know it's not where you'd probably choose to live, but it'll teach you a lot about life. Plus, your father can be very persuasive."

I fight to keep my cheeks flaming at the suggestion of everything that house will teach me.

I know the real reason Mum was so keen to agree to Dad's plans was the financial burden of putting me through university. This way, I might have to move in with them, but he's paying for everything plus giving me hands-on experience with the business. Most parents would have a hard time turning down that kind of opportunity for their child.

My life pretty much carried on normally when Dad met Jenny. It wasn't until they married that things started to change. Suddenly, Dad enrolled me into the same school Ben went to for sixth form, expressing their delight with Ben's education and that it would give me the best start in life despite the cost. I'd agreed because I hated my school and the thought of spending another two years there didn't really appeal to me. It was obvious I'd get more out of two years at a private school, and I was up for a new challenge. I wasn't aware that by agreeing, I basically gave him permission to control my education and life from there on out.

I can't really complain. I finished my two years with a whole set of As, acceptance into an incredible university, and my best friend.

"What's that look for?" Mum asks, noticing my slight embarrassment.

"I need to ask a massive favour of you. I'm not sure you're going to like it."

"Go on..." she encourages.

Blowing out a breath and casting my eyes to the other side of the kitchen, I prepare to tell Mum what's going on. "Dad and Jenny are going away this weekend and Dad wants me to stay with you, but..."

"But..."

"I've got plans that involve me staying there."

"Oh, have you met someone?" she asks excitedly.

"Yes...no—I don't really know."

"Lauren, you know I'd never stop you from having fun." The wink she gives me makes me want to curl up into a ball in embarrassment. "I don't understand the issue."

"He's already threatened to check up on me that I'm staying with you, so I need you to tell him I am."

"But why doesn't he want you staying there—"

I watch as the penny suddenly drops.

"Lauren, who's the boy you've met?"

Staring at her, I bite down on the inside of my lip. Once I say his name, I'm not going to be able to take it back. I'm terrified that Mum will think less of me, or won't approve—or worse, have the same opinion as Dad about Ben.

"It's..."

"It's..." she prompts, her eyebrows almost at her hairline.

"Ben," I whisper, looking down at the floor and cringing as I wait for her reaction.

"Jesus, Lauren," she breathes. When I look up, she's swallowing a giant gulp of wine. Her eyes find mine and I'm surprised when I see them crinkle with amusement at the sides. "*Now* I see your issue. Does your father know?"

"No. He already hates Ben. I overheard an argument between the two of them last night. I've never heard Dad like that before. He threatened to kill him if he so much as touched me."

Mum slouches back in her chair as she digests all this information and takes another sip of wine before she speaks. "Lauren, you're a bright young woman. I know you didn't come here for me to give you the '*but he's your stepbrother*' speech. I have every confidence that you've considered every angle of this situation and don't need a lecture from me. Having said that—" I can't help the groan that falls from my lips. "Are you sure he's worth it? Because I can guarantee you that when this gets out—and it will, you mark my words—all hell's going to break loose. I've no idea the goings-on in that house or their relationship, because I've tried my best to take a huge step back, but I do know there are issues, and I've no doubt your Dad's controlling streak is probably to blame. He wants what's best for you, and he's not afraid to bulldoze his way through others to make that happen." Mum's face saddens and I know all too well that she's talking from experience. "So, I'll ask again: Is he really worth the consequences of what happens when your father finds out what's been going on under his own roof?"

The silence stretches out between us as images of our time together run through my head. My insides flutter as I remember how he makes me feel when we're together, when he touches me. "Yes," I state. "He is."

"I remember what it was like to be young and in love," Mum says with a dreamy look on her face.

"I never said I was in love with him."

"No, but you're my daughter through and through, and looking into your eyes right now, it's like staring into a mirror and seeing the eighteen-year-old version of myself."

"What would you say to her now?" I ask, knowing exactly what happened with the man she fell in love with at only eighteen.

She chuckles to herself before trying to form her answer. "I'd love to tell her that she's young, foolish, and doesn't know what love is. But, in reality, your heart doesn't care how old you are, and it also doesn't have a crystal ball. So, the man I thought was my knight in shining armour turned out to be a cheating control freak, but I know plenty of people who are still very happily married to those they met as a teenager. My first love might not have turned out to be the man of my dreams, but he gave me many things, one of which I could never ever regret." Taking my hand, she stares at me through teary eyes. "If I had my time again, I think my advice would be to love as hard and as much as you can while you have it. Life is unpredictable and you never know when it might be taken away from you. You have to trust what your heart's telling you, Lauren. If you don't, you risk making a mistake you could regret for the rest of your life."

CHAPTER EIGHT

MUM'S WORDS run through my head all evening. It's almost a distraction from the fact that I know I'm not going to see Ben tonight. He told me earlier that he was going to stay away, and I've no reason to think he's changed his mind, as much as I might want him to.

After unpacking everything I bought earlier in the day, I run myself a bath, pour in the luxury bubbles I picked up, cover my face in a mask, and try to relax. Ben never said the words, but I'm assuming he's intending to go all the way this weekend, and I want to be as prepared as possible.

I scrub every inch of my body, shave and wax every hair I can find, and spend forever perfecting my eyebrows and nails. If I had more time, I'd get them done professionally, but this weekend has been kind of sprung on me so this will have to do.

It's long past midnight when I eventually get into bed. Just thinking about having a whole weekend alone with him has my heart pounding and excitement coursing through my veins.

I lie there, tossing and turning, but the anticipation of what the next few days might hold, plus listening for him to come home, stops any sleep I was hoping to get from coming. So much for being rejuvenated for tomorrow.

My body must have given up at some point because, when my alarm goes off the next morning, I almost jump out of bed in fright. I'm usually awake before it, so this is unusual.

It's not until I sit up that everything comes back to me. Butterflies take flight as I try to imagine what it's going to be like...Just the two of us doing whatever we want to do.

I sit there for way too long. I can't believe what time it is once I come back to myself, and I end up rushing around as I get ready to leave for work. It's only early, but already the heat of the summer morning has me melting as I run around, trying not to be late.

Dad's car has already gone when I look out the window. I debate driving myself so I can be home faster, but if I can't get parked, it'll be a nightmare. Deciding the best thing to do would be to get the tube, I slide on a pair of ballet pumps, pull my bag over my shoulder, and set about leaving the house. The next time I'm here, it's just going to be the two of us.

I get a knowing smile from Erica when I make it to the office, but thankfully the day passes without her saying anything. Dad spends a few hours locked away in his office before making a show of packing up while everyone else is busy. He can be a real arsehole when he wants to be. I've often wondered what my mum saw in him when she was only eighteen. Whatever it was, she clearly fell fast and hard if her words to me last night are anything to go by.

"Are you all set for the weekend?" he asks when he stops by my desk on the way out.

"Sure am." I smile sweetly at him, hoping it's enough to convince him that I won't be spending the weekend doing unspeakable things with his stepson. The reality of it almost has me laughing, but I manage to keep a lid on my emotions.

"I fully intend to check in with your mother later today to make sure."

"It's not necessary, Dad. We've got the weekend all planned." He stares at me for a few seconds as if he'll be able to see the evidence of my lie in my eyes. He must be happy with what's reflected back at him, because he wishes me a good weekend and marches from the office.

"Staying with your mum, my arse," Erica whispers when she comes to a stop in front of my desk to collect my mug.

I fight to keep my smile in, but the second I look up and see amusement dancing in her eyes, I can't help but let it slip.

"I hope you know what you're doing, Lauren, because you sure are playing with fire."

Her parting words hinder my excitement a bit, but I push it to one side. Nothing is going to ruin this weekend. Nothing.

WHEN I STEP foot outside the office later that afternoon, the last thing I expect to find is a guy getting out of a taxi, asking if I'm Lauren. I hesitate because wanting nothing to ruin this weekend includes not being abducted by a taxi driver.

"Ben booked me for you." He rattles off my home address and shows his ID when I still look a little sceptical. Eventually, I climb into the back of the car.

I'm grateful the second the air conditioning hits me because the humidity today is through the roof.

The driver tries making polite conversation, but he soon learns that I'm really not in the mood. I just want to get home to find out if Ben's there waiting for me. I bloody hope so.

My stomach flips when I see his car parked alongside mine in the driveway as the taxi pulls to a stop.

"How much do I owe you?" I ask in a rush, impatient to get out.

"Nothing. He's already paid."

"Okay, well, thank you."

"Have a good weekend." I don't have time to return the sentiment because I slam the door before running towards the house.

I had this crazy fantasy of him sweeping me off my feet the second I walk through the door, so when he's not there, a little disappointment threatens to take hold. That is, until I see a Post-It note stuck to the mirror.

Go to your room x

Plucking it from the glass, I follow the instructions and head upstairs. When I open the door, the first thing I spot is a bag on my bed with another Post-It stuck to it.

Wear me x

My hands shake as I pull the bag open and let the contents drop to the bed. Unfolding the fabric, I find a floral maxi dress, a man's zip-up hoodie, and a jewellery box.

Quickly stripping out of my work clothes, I have a very quick shower before smothering myself in my favourite moisturiser. I pull one set of the lingerie I bought yesterday from the drawer and wrap myself in the soft lace before sliding my new dress up my body. It fits perfectly and shows off just the right amount of cleavage—I assume that's on purpose. Finally, I slide my feet into a pair of flip-flops and pull the lid off the jewellery box. My breath catches when I see the two heart charms hanging from the dainty silver chain. I rush to put it on and hold the two hearts between my fingertips, taking a deep breath to prepare myself to go and find him.

When I get to the bottom of the stairs, the house is still in silence. Getting impatient, I begin checking each room downstairs, but I come up short. It's not until I get to the final room, the kitchen, that I start to understand.

Walking over to the sliding doors, I can't believe my eyes. It's still light out, but I can easily see all the fairy lights hanging from the trees over the garden. Candles cover the decking and table, and the scent of vanilla mixes with the barbeque and fills my nose, making my stomach rumble. The furniture is all set up with cushions and the giant swing seat has a blanket thrown over the back.

As I round the corner, I find the best sight in the world. Ben's stood in front of the barbeque wearing a pair of dark jeans and a white t-shirt. His feet are bare, his hair still damp from the shower.

Something inside me clenches at the sight and I stand, staring, trying to commit exactly how he looks right now to my memory.

"Feel free to take a picture," he says, when he realises I'm frozen.

"Sorry, you just look—"

"Nowhere near as good as you." His wide strides quickly eat the space between us and in seconds I'm in his arms, his lips on mine. My entire body sags against him. It's been too long.

His tongue sweeps into my mouth and he kisses me like he hasn't in months, not hours.

"Missed you," he mumbles against my jaw as he kisses a trail towards my neck. My response is just a moan of pleasure as he licks at the sensitive skin below my ear. My body melts under his touch and I want nothing more than to give myself over to him. I want him to completely own me.

Hearing a bang in the distance, I stiffen. "They've definitely gone, right?"

"Yep. It's just me and you, baby."

A thrill rushes through me and I reach for him again. Twisting the fabric of his t-shirt in my hands, I pull him flush against me, desperate to feel his hard body against mine.

We stand and kiss on the decking for the longest time. I can't get enough. When he pulls back, my lips are swollen and sore, but I can't think of anything better.

"We've got all weekend; we don't need to rush," he says with a laugh when I refuse to let him go. "I should feed you first, anyway. I've got a suspicion you're going to need sustenance." His eyes drop to my necklace and my exposed cleavage, and I watch them darken even further as his tongue comes out to wet his bottom lip. My entire body throbs with my need for him, but nowhere more than between my legs. It's bordering on uncomfortable.

"Stop looking at me like that or I'll forget all about the dinner."

"Would that be such a bad thing?"

"Lauren," he half moans, half laughs. "I'm trying

to do this properly. Treat you right." For the first time ever, he seems so unsure of himself. It's just another reminder that the bad boy image he shows everyone is just an act. Underneath it all is a kind and gentle man who wants to be loved like everyone else.

"You're doing perfect," I say, dropping a kiss to the side of his neck. Intertwining our fingers, I pull him back over to the barbeque. "So, what are we cooking?"

"What *aren't* we cooking? I wasn't sure what you liked, so I went a little crazy." Lifting the lid, I see that he's not lying. Everything you could possibly want at a barbeque is laid on the bars beginning to cook. "And I made mojitos. That's what you drink, right?"

"Stop worrying. This is perfect. *You're* perfect."

Twisting us around, he pulls me in front of him and wraps his arms around my waist. I look out at the garden beyond as Ben breathes me in. "I'm far from that."

"Not to me." I feel his smile against my head and my heart beats that little bit faster. Mum's words from last night hit me. *"I remember what it was like to be young and in love."*

Was she right? Is this what falling in love feels like?

Turning me once again, he walks me backwards

until my back bumps against the railing. His hips press against mine, and his arousal is impossible to miss. My eyes widen in surprise. I've barely touched him.

"You've no idea how badly I need you."

"I think I do. How long until dinner starts burning?"

"Probably ten minutes. Why?"

With the railing at my back and him at my front, I manage to lower myself to my knees. Ben's eyes follow my every move. The blue turns almost black and his lids hang heavy with lust.

"Lauren," he moans when I reach out and undo the button on his jeans. I've no idea if it was meant to be a demand to stop or words of encouragement, but now I've got the idea in my head, there's no way I'm not tasting him right now.

I feel his stare as I pull his jeans and boxers down his thighs, but I can't tear my eyes away from his cock as it springs free.

His body shudders as I wrap my hand around him. "Fucking hell," he groans. His pleasure spurs me on. I lean forward slightly and gently lick at the end of him. His hips thrust forward with his need for more, but I continue teasing him. "Jesus fucking Christ, Lauren. Shit. Argh," he moans when I suck him as far into my mouth as he'll go.

His taste fills my mouth as I pull back and slowly flick my tongue around him once more.

I start to smell burning coming from the barbeque behind us when I reach up and cup his balls in my hand. He moans loudly above me once again before his warning comes. Ignoring it, I suck him harder. His cock twitches and his entire body stills as his cum lands on my tongue.

Once he's finished, I sit back and lick my lips. I can still feel his stare burning the top of my head, and when I look up, my breath catches. The desire in his eyes, his parted lips as he pants out his increased breaths—it all has my thighs clenching.

"Our first time's going to be everything you deserve, but fuck if I don't want to bend you over that railing right this fucking second."

Standing back to full height, I allow my lips to brush his. "Ben..." His lids lower once again, expecting me to say something sexual, but instead I whisper, "Put your cock away. The dinner's burning."

Barking out a laugh that fills me with warmth, he quickly does as I suggest.

Sitting down on one of the chairs, I pour myself a mojito from the jug and enjoy watching him cook. Music softly plays on a speaker set up on the table, the birds sing in the trees above, and the evening sun warms my skin. I can't think of a better way to spend tonight.

"What?" Ben asks when I look over at him with a smile on my face.

"Thank you for this."

"You're more than welcome. Where does your dad think you're spending the weekend?" he asks as he brings over a plate piled high with food.

"At Mum's."

"I thought he said he'd ring to check?"

"He probably will. But Mum's on our side."

Pausing halfway through assembling his burger, he looks up at me, confusion filling his eyes. "You... told her? About us?"

"I did."

"What did she say?"

"That if I think you're important enough to risk it, she'll support my decision."

"Wow, that's..." He trails off, deep in thought, and I can only imagine he's wondering want Jenny would make of all of this.

"She's pretty incredible."

"She sounds it. It's a shame everyone doesn't think like her."

"Everything's going to be okay," I say when a sad expression falls over his face.

He opens his mouth to respond but must think

better of it. "Let's forget about all of that for now and just enjoy our weekend."

"Sounds like a perfect plan."

Silence surrounds us as we eat, my concerns after that brief conversation at the forefront of my mind.

THE NIGHT GOES by all too quickly and, before I know it, we're sitting in the dark under the twinkling lights Ben strung up in the trees. Most of the candles have long burnt out and we've drunk our way through the mojito jug. I'm feeling suitably full from all of Ben's incredible cooking and buzzed from the slightly too strong cocktail.

"You're freezing. Shall we go in?" We've been cuddled up on the swing, under the blanket for ages, chatting away and just enjoying each other's company. Nerves and excitement for what's to come hit me all at once. "We don't have to do anything if you're not ready. As long as you're beside me, that's all I need."

Cupping his stubble-covered cheeks, I pull his lips to mine. "Liar," I say with a laugh. I go to kiss him to show him I want to give him everything, but he places his hands on my shoulders, stopping me.

"I'm deadly serious, Lauren. If you're not ready—"

"Shut up." Throwing my leg over his lap, I get settled and resume my earlier kiss. I've no intention of this night ending here. I've held on to my V card until I found the right guy, and I'm so bloody glad I did because I can't imagine anything more perfect than this.

"Go and get yourself comfortable upstairs. I'll be right up," he says between kisses to my neck.

I'm hesitant to move, too content to be sitting across his lap with his hands on me. When he realises I'm not going anywhere, he lifts me and places me on my feet. His biceps bulge as he takes my weight and the sight only increases my need to have his naked, hot, smooth skin pressed up against mine.

"Go," he says again with a tap to my arse.

Walking across the deck, I try to put as much sass into it as possible. I know his eyes are on me. I can feel them.

When I get to the sliding doors, I look back over my shoulder. Exactly as I expect, his eyes are focused on my arse. Realising I've stopped, he lifts his gaze and finds mine. The promise within his dark eyes has tingles racing through me.

I eventually manage to tear myself away from him and head towards my bedroom. Now that I'm moving, it hits me just how tipsy I actually am. My head spins as I wobble my way up the stairs. I'm too consumed with how Ben makes me feel when he's around to put much thought into the effects of the alcohol.

I've no idea how long I've got, so I quickly make use of the bathroom and brush my teeth. I feel like a different person when I look at myself in the mirror. My eyes are bright and sparkling and my skin has a glow I don't think I've ever seen on myself before.

Hearing a bang from downstairs brings me back to the here and now, and my heart thunders in my chest. This small amount of distance between us has allowed my nerves to creep in. They're easy to forget when Ben's got his hands on me. My body takes over and tells me exactly what I need. *Allowing me this alone time was dangerous,* I laugh to myself as I try to force my anxiety down.

I'm running a brush through my hair when I hear his footsteps pounding up the stairs. My body temperature spikes, my heart races, and my hands begin to tremble. But the second the door opens and my eyes find his, all of that vanishes.

It's just the two of us. No worries or concerns, no outside influences. Just me, him, and this explosive thing between us.

"Lauren," he breathes, running his eyes down the

length of me. Tingles that had started to disappear suddenly hit me full force once again.

Stepping up to me, he takes my hand and pulls me over to the bed. I lie down and rest my head on my pillow at his encouragement. Our eyes meet and our breaths mingle, our bodies just inches apart.

I flinch when his warm hand lands on my cheek where I'm so lost in his eyes. I wasn't expecting this. I had visions of him stripping me bare the second he entered the room and doing wicked things to me. Instead, his face is full of emotion, almost to the point where I'm concerned.

"You make all of this so much easier, Lauren," he whispers, and my breath catches at the honesty in his words. "You make everything seem worthwhile again. I've been walking through life in a haze for a long time, but for the first time in years I'm suddenly seeing things clearly. I feel like I have a home again, I feel like I belong." Tears burn my eyes. Until now, I had no idea if this crazy connection I felt with him was one-sided, but, if anything, it seems like it means even more to him.

"You make me want to do something about this bullshit life I've been living. You give me a reason to fight. To fight for what's right. To fight for what I deserve." He pauses and his eyes run over every inch of my face. "I had no idea I was looking for something, and I really had no clue that I was going to find what I so desperately needed in my own house. But here you are, like a guardian fucking angel. I promise you, I'm going to do whatever it takes to prove I'm worthy of you, to protect you, to keep you...to be yours."

The strength behind his words renders me speechless. He must sense it because nothing more is said as he closes the space between us and presses his lips to mine.

He kisses me for hours, his hands running over every clothed inch of me, but he never pushes for more. I thought I'd be disappointed, but I can't have imagined anything more perfect. It was exactly what both of us needed after his confession.

CHAPTER NINE

I WAKE UP FEELING HOT. I soon understand why when I feel the soft brush of Ben's lips across my collarbone.

"Good morning," I whisper, but it comes out more like a breathy moan.

"It sure is, baby."

Tearing my eyes open, I find him staring down at me, lust filling his eyes. Gone is last night's emotion, only to be replaced by a hunger I recognise well. It causes my insides to clench.

I go to sit myself up but his hand on my ribs stops me. "Lie back. I've got things I want to do to you—and trust me, they can't wait."

"Okay," I breathe, but I'm not sure he hears as he drops his lips back to my skin. He kisses down my chest and over the swell of my breasts. When he gets to the fabric of the dress I'm still wearing, he tucks his finger under the edge and pulls it back.

"Jesus," he moans when he sees the lace bra I chose especially for him. Lifting his hands to my shoulders, he slips the straps of my dress down my arms before pulling it down my body. His eyes feast on every bit of skin he reveals.

After dropping the fabric to the floor, he stands back and stares. Tingles follow his eyes as he runs them over every inch of me. My chest heaves, my breasts strain against the lace covering them, and my core aches.

"Sweet Jesus. You look fucking sinful. What are you doing to me?"

If he's waiting for a response, he doesn't show it. Instead, he pulls his t-shirt over his head and drops it to the floor, followed by his jeans and boxers, allowing me my first look at all of him. Suddenly, I understand his fascination with my body a few seconds ago, because my eyes are glued to him. I follow the definition of his abs, down his v lines to his hard cock bobbing in front of him. My mouth waters.

He doesn't allow me any longer to appreciate the view because, after dragging my knickers down, he crawls back onto the bed and starts kissing down my leg. My thighs quiver when he makes it to my core.

"So fucking sweet," he murmurs, running his nose against my sensitive skin.

"Please, Ben. I need—" My words are cut off when his tongue connects with my clit.

It's like he can read my body and knows exactly what's going to have me racing towards my release. He sucks hard on my clit before sliding one, then two, fingers inside me.

I pant and moan his name, my hands twisting in the sheet beneath me as I reach the point of no return. He does something with his fingers and I'm falling. I cry out as my orgasm races through me, every part of my body pulsing with pleasure.

He looks smug when he pulls back and stares at me. "I don't want to know how you got so good at that," I say with a laugh.

His face pales slightly before saying, "I'm only going to get better with all the practice I'm expecting to have."

My thighs clench despite the fact that he's just shattered me into a million pieces.

After reaching down to his discarded clothes, Ben drops a little silver square to the bed and kisses his way up my body.

"You ready for this?" I swallow my nerves and nod. He can see right through my act because his palm lands on my cheek and his soft eyes hold mine. "If you're not, just tell me. We don't have to."

"No. No, I want this. I want you. Please, Ben. Just be...just be gentle?" I feel ridiculous asking, but I can't help the words falling from my mouth.

"I promise to never be anything but, baby."

I watch as he rolls the condom over his length and settles himself between my thighs. He presses the tip against my clit, his eyes locked on mine. He's waiting for me to change my mind, but it won't happen.

"I want you, Ben. I want you to be my first." I swear my words make his chest puff out a little. He holds our connection as he finds my entrance and slowly pushes inside me. Thanks to his talented mouth, I'm ready for him.

He feels huge as he slides into me, and I shift my hips as I try to adjust to the alien sensation—until he seems to hit a brick wall and I know what's going to come next is going to hurt like hell.

Dropping forward, he nuzzles his face into my neck. "I hate to do this," he whispers, "but I promise to make it so worth it."

The heat of his body pressing down on mine feels out of this world. I need this. I need more of him.

"Do it," I say, sounding more confident than I

feel. Running my hands down his back, I squeeze his arse to give him a little encouragement.

He sucks the sensitive skin below my ear into his mouth. I'm just enjoying the tingles it causes when he thrusts his hips forward.

He doesn't move again as I moan in pain. "I'm sorry, I'm sorry," he whispers. He sounds mortified to have hurt me.

Pulling his head from my neck, I force him to look at me. "Hey, it's okay." I go to run my thumb over his bottom lip, but he captures it and sucks it into his mouth. His earlier hunger seeps back into his features and I flex my hips, showing him that I'm okay. I'm actually better than okay; we're connected in the most intimate way possible, and I can't think of anything better.

"You sure?"

"Let me feel you. Please." He rolls his hips and the pain that was so strong only moments ago dissipates, the incredible feeling of him moving inside me taking over.

"Fucking hell, you're so tight. I hope you weren't expecting this to last long," he moans before dropping down to kiss me.

When his pace starts increasing, I know he's nearing the end and I'm desperate to experience it.

"Jesus, Lauren, I'm going to come so fucking

hard," he grunts, the words filling me with warmth. Threading his fingers into my hair, his hips move fast, then faster. His other hand slips down until he presses his fingertips against my sensitive clit. My entire body arches from the bed at the contact. "Fuck."

With his fingers teasing my clit and his length hitting some magical place inside me, it's not long before he pushes me over the edge and I come with his name a soft moan on my lips. Seconds later, he growls above me before I feel his cock twitch violently inside me. He roars his release and the look on his face as he does is something I'll never forget. Everything that usually drags him down has gone, and he's lost to the pleasure. Pleasure that I am able to give him. My heart swells and I fear I'm falling way too hard, way too fast. I'm trying not to think about the future because I know that, no matter what, it's going to be a challenge.

"Holy shit, Lauren," he pants, falling down at my side, his breath rushing over my face as he tries to catch it.

"Good?" I hate the anxiety that creeps into my voice.

"Good?" He repeats with a laugh. "That was fucking mind-blowing. I'm already craving more." His lips meet mine as his warm hand slides around my back, tickling my hypersensitive skin before flicking the clasp on my bra. I'd totally forgotten I was still wearing it.

Pulling back from my lips, he ducks his head and pulls one of my nipples into his mouth. A sigh falls from my lips as another ball of sensation explodes within me.

"Stop it," he says with a laugh after releasing my nipple with a pop. "I don't need any encouragement to spend all day inside you."

"That doesn't sound like a bad way to spend today," I admit.

"No, but you need a rest before we go again." My heart swells once again at his thoughtfulness. "What? Why are you looking at me like that?"

"I like you." My cheeks heat at my admission, and if it wasn't for the incredible smile that erupts across Ben's face, I might have looked away.

"I like you too, Lauren. *A lot.*"

"COME ON," he says, intertwining our hands and pulling me from the bed after kissing me breathless.

"You want me to..." I flick a glance down at his hard cock and raise an eyebrow.

"More than I probably should admit. But this is about you, not me."

I follow him into my ensuite, my mouth dropping open when I take in the flickering candles that cover every available surface. Walking straight up to the bath, he climbs in and encourages me to follow. In seconds, soothing bubbles and Ben's arms surround me. I lie back against his chest and sigh.

"I hope that's a good sigh."

"Mmm...it is. I don't think I've ever been this relaxed."

"Every morning should start with orgasms, don't you think?"

"As long as they're delivered by you."

He goes silent behind me. I can feel the sudden tension in his muscles. Sitting up, sloshing water everywhere, I turn and straddle him. I hate not being able to see his face.

"What's wrong?" He tries looking away, but I bring his face back to me. "Ben?"

"I'm sorry; it's nothing."

"It's not nothing. You can tell me, whatever it is." Sliding my hand around the back of his neck, I tilt and drop a quick kiss to his lips.

"It's just...this is so incredible." My breath catches when he places his hand over my heart.

"You're so incredible. But..." He lets out a pained breath.

"What happens when we're caught?" I finish for him.

"Yeah," he agrees sadly.

"Enough," I snap, a little too harshly if his wide eyes are anything to go by. "We've got plenty of time to worry about that. But right now, we've got an empty house all to ourselves. The most important thing to worry about is what we're going to do for the next twenty-four hours."

"Or how many times I can make you come."

"Hmm...that, too. What did you have planned?"

"Nothing past last night. What did you want to do?"

"Nothing sounds perfect. Well, maybe not totally nothing." Sitting back between his legs, I slide my hand up his thigh, giggling to myself when it makes his cock twitch. Taking him in my hand, I slowly slide it up and down, all the while watching Ben's eyes roll back in pleasure. Yeah, I think this could be the perfect way to spend the weekend.

Once the water's cold, we both climb out of the bath and set about with whatever we're going to do. Ben walks over to the window and pulls the curtains back. "How about just chilling out in the garden? I've got plenty of food left over from last night. We could barbeque again later."

"Sounds perfect." Pulling open a drawer, I rummage around for a bikini.

"What's that for?" he asks, eyeing the small bit of red fabric in my hands.

"Sunbathing?" The look on his face as he stares at it makes the word come out like a question.

"Not necessary." The fabric is snatched from my hands and shoved back into the drawer.

"Ben, I'm not walking around all day naked."

"Why not? No one will see you but me." I try to come up with a reasonable argument other than I don't want to, but the moment I see the fire in his eyes, all thoughts leave my head. Running my eyes down the chiselled planes of his abs, I realise it's not such a bad idea. "And it means I can have you any time I want."

We don't leave my bedroom for at least another hour, and I have a feeling today is going to be exhausting in a very, very good way.

Thankfully, he relents on me wearing clothes, so as we walk hand in hand into the kitchen, I'm wearing my bikini and a pair of hot pants and he's looking like a freaking swimwear model in his low-hanging board shorts.

"What do you want for breakfast?" he asks after kick-starting both the kettle and the coffee machine.

"Hmm...cake."

"Cake?" he asks with a laugh.

"Why not? This weekend is about indulging, so what's more indulgent than cake for breakfast?"

"Good point. I'm pretty sure there's no cake in this house."

"There's stuff to make one, though." I know for a fact that there's everything we'll need at the back of the larder cupboard, because I bought it and put it there a couple of weeks ago.

"I haven't made a cake since Food Tech in year 9, and that was a disaster!"

"It's a good job you've got an excellent teacher, then."

"I'm sensing this lesson will be a little different than the one I'm remembering." His eyes drop to my barely clothed body, and he leisurely takes in every inch. "Definitely better," he mutters quietly while rearranging himself in his shorts.

"Come on, let's bake," I say, grabbing his hand and pulling him over to the counter. Finding the scales in the darkest part of the bottom cupboard, I give them a clean before instructing Ben to weigh out the correct amounts.

"Can't we just guess?"

"No. Baking is a science."

"I always preferred sex ed."

"You're a nightmare." I sit myself up on the island counter as Ben beats the eggs and folds in the flour exactly as instructed. "Don't forget the cocoa powder." I pop the top off and pull at the foil beneath. I put a little more force into it than necessary and, in seconds, almost a full tub of cocoa powder covers my boobs and thighs as well as the counter and the floor.

"You need a hand?" Ben asks, his eyes darkening as he looks at my dirty chest.

"No, I've got it." I go to dust it off but he captures my wrist before I get the chance.

"Let me." His head drops forward before his tongue licks the powder from my breast.

"That's going to be—"

"Ew, that tastes nothing like chocolate," he says, pulling back with his lips curled in disgust. "I know what will make it better."

"Ben, no!" I squeal when he reaches into the icing sugar and grabs a handful. The white dust is thrown just as I jump down from the counter. Icing sugar surrounds me. Every breath tastes sweet as it begins to settle on my skin. "I can't believe you just did that."

Before I have a chance to move, Ben's hands slide

around my waist and I'm pulled against him. His lips go to my neck and he licks a trail down to the valley between my breasts. "So much better than cake," he mumbles as he continues licking.

My nipples pebble against the thin fabric of my bikini top and heat floods my core.

"Oh…I think you got a little bit…" Pulling the cup from my breast, I watch as Ben licks around my nipple before sucking it deep into his mouth. My head falls back as my clit starts to pound.

"Oh my God," I whimper as he swaps to the other side and gives it the same treatment.

"Don't move," he demands. The serious look in his eyes means I don't argue. I stand, surrounded by cocoa powder and icing sugar dust with my breasts on show while Ben adds all that's left of the cocoa powder into the cake mix. "Hey, I told you to stay there," he complains when I begin dragging my nails down his back. I can't help but smile when his skin pricks with goosebumps and his entire body shudders.

"Sorry, I couldn't help myself." I slide my hands around to his stomach as he begins pouring the mixture into the tins I lined earlier.

"Fuck, Lauren," he complains when I slip one hand under the waistband of his shorts and wrap my hand around him. He manages to flinch and miss the tin. Reaching out, I run my finger through the mixture and bring it up to his lips. "Suck," I demand, praying my voice sounds as sexy as I hope it does.

"Mmm," he moans as he laps at my finger, licking off every bit of the mixture. "I think I've got an idea for where I want to eat the rest of this from." My insides clench at the suggestion. "How...how long do these take?" he stutters when I start stroking him.

"About twenty minutes."

"That should be enough time."

"Enough time for what?" Slipping away from my grasp, be pulls the oven door open and slides the two tins inside. Then, he turns to me. His eyes are dark and hungry as they drop from mine and take in my curves. Reaching out, he pops the buttons on my shorts and pushes them down my thighs. Wiggling my hips, I get them to fall to my feet and step out while he pulls at the ties around my back and at my hips. In seconds, the fabric flutters to the floor and I'm stood bare before him, bar the cocoa powder and icing sugar clinging to my skin.

After dropping his own shorts, he grabs my waist and lifts. I have no choice but to sit on the edge of the counter.

"Lie back," he demands. I wince when my back hits the cold marble beneath me, but it's soon forgotten when I feel Ben's breath tickle my sensitive skin.

Propping myself up on my elbows, I watch as Ben feasts on me. The fact that we're out in the open in the middle of our parents' house only helps push me closer to my orgasm.

His lids flutter open, and his intense eyes land on mine. My heart flips over. I'm totally consumed by this man.

He slides two fingers deep inside me, his tongue continuing to torture my clit, and I fall over the edge, my body twitching and convulsing on top of the counter.

Pulling back, Ben wipes his mouth with the back of his hand before taking himself in his hand. He teases my sensitive clit, then drops to find my entrance. "How sore are you?"

"Not sore enough to stop you."

In one quick thrust, he's inside me.

He grunts and stills for a beat. His eyes find mine and I swear I can see everything he's feeling inside them.

"I'm going to fuck you in every room of this house, Lauren." I'm not sure if it's a warning, a promise, or just a big *fuck you* to my dad, but in this moment I really don't care. I also don't have any argument because sex in every room sounds pretty incredible.

"What are you doing?" I ask the second he pulls out of me. I'm learning his body quickly and I know he's about to come.

"No...condom," he grunts before the heat of his cum lands on me.

Fuck, that's hot, I think as I watch the muscles in his neck and shoulders strain as he works his cock.

"It's okay. I'm on the pill," I admit once he's finished.

"We need to be safe," is all he says. I can't agree more. An accidental pregnancy is the last thing we need.

"I need a shower," I say with a laugh, looking down at my body.

"That sounds like a plan." In seconds, I'm in his arms and we're heading for the stairs.

My legs are still wrapped around his waist as he leans in and turns the water on. Once it's warm, he stands us under the powerful spray. Ben slides me down his body as the water begins to wash away the sticky mess covering both of us.

"Turn around," he whispers in my ear, and before I know what's happening, his hands are in my hair and the scent of my shampoo fills the small space around us.

"Oh my God. So good," I moan as he massages my scalp.

"You like my fingers, don't you, baby?"

"You're so cheesy," I laugh.

Once he's finished with my hair, his talented fingers skim over every inch of me, removing the evidence of our attempt at baking— "Shit, the cake!"

"Fuck. I'll go." Quickly rinsing off the bubbles from his body, Ben jumps out of the shower, wraps a towel around his waist, and runs from the room.

I follow a few minutes after. The second I open the bathroom door, I can smell burning.

"Safe to say that's fucked," Ben says with a laugh when he reappears. Suddenly, I couldn't care less about the cake; he's still just got the towel wrapped around him and droplets of water running down his pecs and abs. I think it might be my favourite look on him.

"Keep looking at me like that and you might never leave this room."

"I can think of much worse things."

"Me too. But we'll save that for another day. Get dressed."

"WHERE ARE WE GOING?" I ask as we step out of the front door.

"You wanted cake, and we failed miserably at making one, so I thought I'd treat you instead."

Not being able to argue with his idea, I fall into step beside him as he walks us past both our cars and out onto the street.

"Oh my God, I love this place," I squeal as Ben leads me into the dessert-only restaurant not that far from home. The sweet smell has my mouth watering the second we enter.

"Will this fix your cake craving?"

"Just a little bit. The only problem is choosing."

Both of us indulge in way too many calories by the time we pay and make our way home...but I figure we've already exerted ourselves enough to get away with it.

CHAPTER TEN

"LAUREN, WAKE UP." Ben's soft voice filters through my sleep-fogged brain and I pry my eyes open to look at him. The smile he greets me with melts my heart, but it doesn't stop me feeling like I should be fast asleep right now.

"What time is it?"

"Early. Come on, get up. There's something I want to show you."

Lifting my heavy head, I take in the numbers on my alarm clock. "Why the hell are you dragging me out of bed at three-thirty in the morning?"

"It'll be worth it, I promise." There are very few things that will make this worth it, but I refrain from voicing my concerns because Ben seems excited. "Here, get dressed." A pair of jeans and the hoodie he gave me gets thrown onto the bed, and after finding myself some underwear, I pull them on.

Once dressed, Ben takes my hand and leads me out to his car. It's still dark out and the street is in silence. As we drive through the city of London, it's quieter than I ever thought I'd experience—although there are still way too many people out at this hour, in my opinion.

"Where are we going?" I ask, desperately trying to keep my eyes open.

"Just wait."

I vaguely recognise parts of our journey, so when he pulls up into the deserted car park he brought me to after our first date, I'm not surprised.

"I should probably tell you now that I'm not really interested in any kinky shit that might go down in this place after dark."

Ben barks out a laugh. "Don't worry, I have no intention of allowing anyone to watch through the window. That's not why we're here."

"Why *are* we here?"

"For that," he says pointing to where the sun is just beginning to creep over the horizon in the distance.

"Oh." I'm gobsmacked that bad boy Ben has brought me to watch the sunrise. He really does put on a good show for everyone, and I suddenly feel so grateful to have been allowed to see the real him.

"Surprised?" he asks like he can read my mind.

"Yeah."

"It's just so peaceful. My dad first showed me this place. Just being here…" He pauses, and I can feel the emotion he's desperately trying to keep inside. His jaw pops where he grinds his teeth and his hands white-knuckle the steering wheel. "It just makes me feel close to him again."

He was only fourteen when his dad suddenly passed away. I can only imagine how he even began to deal with that. Having heard stories from back then, I know that Jenny totally fell apart, so not only was Ben trying to cope with losing his dad, but he was trying to support his mum at the same time. It's no surprise that, when my dad swooped in not all that long later, they didn't really hit it off. My dad had been working for Johnson & Sons, but as a builder. But it didn't seem to take all that long for him to move into their house and take over the business. It was almost like he was waiting, hoping for an opportunity to arise, and when it did, he swooped in like a knight in shining armour and saved the day.

"Let's get out."

Ben jumps from the car and I quickly follow suit,

meeting him at the front. Resting back against the bonnet, he pulls me against him and places his chin on my shoulder.

We sit in a comfortable silence as we watch the sun rise over London. I feel so serene and secure in his arms as we take in one of the busiest cities coming to life.

I can't stop yawning as we head back into the centre.

"No sleeping yet. We've got more places to go."

"It's dawn on a Sunday morning. Where could we possibly need to go?" When he pulls up outside a McDonalds, I can't really argue. "Okay, yeah. This is a good plan."

We fill ourselves full of McMuffins and caffeine, and by the time we walk out, I'm feeling a little more awake.

To my surprise, Ben walks straight past his car and continues farther down the street.

"Where now?"

"I've got an appointment." I look over at him curiously but he doesn't elaborate. Things start to make sense when he comes to a stop in front of Just Ink, a tattoo studio. "Come on," he says, giving my arm a tug and encouraging me to follow him inside.

"Mornin'," a deep voice booms the second Ben opens the door. When I look up, I'm shocked to see

Danni's older brother, Zach, with his arms out in an over-the-top greeting. "It's been too long, dude," He pulls Ben into a quick man hug and slaps him on the back.

"I know. Things have just been a little crazy. You know Lauren, right?"

"I do. Lookin' good, beautiful."

"Hey," I say, trying to keep my amusement hidden when Ben's muscles tense at Zach's greeting and the way he runs his eyes over me.

"Please tell me you've brought her because she's a blank canvas. I do love a virgin." My cheeks flush and I have to look away.

"She is, but you're not getting your hands on her." Ben says it with a laugh, but the warning in his voice is clear. Zach's eyes widen slightly in understanding before he nods and turns to Ben.

"I'm stuck with you, then, huh?"

"Sorry about that."

"I was hoping that if you were dragging me out of bed this early on Sunday, you might have something a little more exciting for me."

"Shut up and get ready, prick."

The banter between them continues as Zach sets up and Ben gets himself comfortable on the leather reclining chair in the back room. It's clear that these two are closer than I first thought. I knew they were friends in school, but I've never heard either mention the other since.

"What are we adding today?"

"I want a sunrise on my shoulder." I watch as Ben points out exactly what he wants and where.

"Sure thing. We'll have this sleeve done in no time."

I watch Zach ink Ben's skin with fascination. I'm in awe of his talent. He makes it look so easy, but I'm not stupid enough to believe that's actually the case.

"Are you sure I can't tempt you?" Zach asks once he's finished working on Ben. "There's nothing like being a woman's first."

"Enough, Zach," Ben snaps, clearly fed up with his blatant flirting.

Zach puts his hands up in defence as he starts clearing up.

"Maybe another day." Both heads turn towards me. Zach's eyes light up whereas Ben's eyebrows draw together, causing a deep line to form.

"You don't want this arsehole's hands on you, b—"

"You're probably right," I interrupt before he says something he won't be able to take back. I'm not sure it helps when I see the look Zach gives us. "I'll just be out there." Turning on my heel, I walk out of the room to wait in reception.

"Promise me you won't let him put his hands on you," Ben says the second we're back inside his car.

"You do know he's already touched me, right?"

"He's fucking *what?*" Ben's face reddens, the muscles in his shoulders bunch, and his lips press into a thin line.

I have to bite back a smile before I can respond. "Calm down, caveman. He's Danni's brother and caught me when I fell down their stairs once, that's all."

Ben blows out a huge breath and sags back against the seat. "Thank fuck for that."

"I thought you were friends. He's a good guy."

"We are. Doesn't mean I trust him, though."

"But you trust me?"

"Of course. Zach's just...a dog."

I can't help laughing. "And you're not?"

He shoots me a look, but his eyes are full of amusement. "Okay, yeah, I deserve that."

Any reference of him being with plenty of girls before me always has nerves fluttering in my belly, but the moment he reaches over and entwines his fingers with mine, I forget all about the outside world and just focus on this—on us.

AS THE CLOCK TICKS AROUND, I feel Ben starting to pull away from me. The whole weekend has been beyond incredible, but we're both well aware that our time is coming to an end. Dad said they wouldn't be back until this afternoon, but it's barely lunchtime and we're both already on edge.

"Let's watch a film," I suggest in an attempt to take our minds off the inevitable. I've tried to push any thoughts of our reality to the back of my mind as we've enjoyed each other this weekend, but it's never really that far away. What we're doing might feel like the most natural thing in the world to us but, to the outside world, what we're doing is forbidden. As far as most people believe, a relationship between us is wrong.

But is it?

"Lauren, are you even watching?" I flinch when Ben's hand lands on my thigh.

"Sorry, yeah. I just zoned out for a minute."

"Do I need to ask what you were thinking about?"

"No. I just don't know what—"

"We'll figure it out." With his hands on my cheeks and confidence shining from his eyes, I almost believe him.

"How?"

"Honestly, I've no idea. But what I do know is

that I'm not letting anyone get between us. I'm not letting you go, Lauren. You make everything so much lighter. I won't go back into the dark. I can't."

His body looming over me forces me to lie back on the sofa. He presses me into the cushions, his lips landing on mine and his hands trailing over my body.

Everything falls away—our surroundings, my concerns, everything but how I feel for him. It's exciting. It's overwhelming. It's scary as hell. But everything he just said is true, because I'm not giving him up, either.

"Honey, we're home." Jenny's voice rings out through the house loud and clear. Ben jumps into action, scrambling off me and practically flying to the chair at the other end of the room. I watch as he looks around in panic, running his hands through his hair, trying to smooth it down.

"Lauren," he prompts when he spots that I haven't moved.

Pulling myself to a sitting position on the sofa, I also attempt to sort out my hair and calm my racing heart. Dread fills me. I've never heard Jenny shout, let alone loud enough to wake the dead like that.

She knows.

"Did you have a good weekend?" Ben asks when she walks into the living room, looking between the two of us.

"Yes, it was love—"

"Lauren, what are you doing here?" Dad barks when he eventually follows her into the room.

"I...uh...came back this morning."

"Your mum said you were staying for lunch."

"I was, but I had some things that needed doing before work tomorrow, so I came back a little early. Problem?" I ask, jutting my chin out. Fire burns within me; I'm ready to start an argument if he wants to.

Turning towards Ben, his stare holds for a few seconds before he looks back at me. "I really hope not," he mutters before storming from the room.

The three of us stay silent as the sounds of him crashing about in the kitchen filter through. Jenny looks between us once more before muttering her excuse and racing from the room.

"This is bullshit," Ben barks.

Looking up at him, I see all the happiness and relaxation from our time together has gone. He's once again full of anger, and as always, it's directed straight at my dad. Frustration fills me that I have no clue what the issue is, but Ben's made it very clear that he's not going to share. I decide there and then that I need to start working on Dad. I need to get to the bottom of this if there's even a slim chance of this working between us.

"I know but—"

"But what? You have some master plan that you haven't shared that will magically make all of this okay?"

"No, but—"

"I can't do this. I can't sit around and watch you from a distance. I'm outta here."

I don't get the chance to respond, because he's gone. The front door slams and his car squeals out of the driveway.

"Oh, has Ben gone?" Jenny asks, walking in with two mugs in her hand.

"I'm sorry, I've got things I need to do." Biting down on my bottom lip so she can't see it trembling, I race past her and up to my room.

The second I enter, his smell hits me and I'm reminded of every thoughtful and gentle thing he did this weekend. My eyes sting and a lump forms in my throat. It was all so perfect for those few hours. Falling onto my bed, I silently cry for what could be. For what Ben and I could have if the situation was different.

"WHAT'S WRONG?" Dad snaps when the three of us are sat around the dining table later that evening.

Ben still hasn't reappeared, and the messages I've sent him to ask if he's okay have gone unread. I feel sick. How can things go from being so perfect to so fucked up so quickly?

"Nothing," I mutter, shovelling some rice into my mouth.

"Could you at least sound a little grateful, Lauren? Not every kid has it as easy as you."

"I'm not a kid." My eyes find Dad's hard and angry ones across the table, but they do little to douse the fire raging inside me. "I'm not a fucking kid."

"Lauren, do not use—"

"What? Are you going to march me to my room and ground me like a child? I'm an adult. I can make my own choices and live my own life."

"You're eighteen. You don't know what you want, let alone what's right," he roars.

"And you do? How could you possibly know what I want and need? You're too busy controlling everything and everyone around you to have time to notice anything I do." Throwing my fork down on the plate, I push my chair out behind me and race to the door.

"Oh, I notice, Lauren. I fucking notice everything," he seethes as I round the corner.

I'm panting when I lean back against my bedroom door. I can probably count on one hand the number of times I've stood up to my dad, and most of those have been since I moved in.

"Fucking hell," I mutter to myself, pacing back and forth across my room. Knowing I can't sit here stewing, I grab my phone. I've got two options.

"OVER HERE," I hear my best friend shout the second I step foot in our favourite bar.

Looking over, I see she's got our favourite booth and there's already a cocktail pitcher in the centre. "So, you want to tell me what this impromptu drinking session is about?"

"Not really." Grabbing myself a glass, I fill it to the top and allow the cold, sweet margarita to slide down my throat.

"In my experience, it can only be two things. Your parents, or a boy. Now, knowing what your dad's like, it's probably him, but for argument's sake, let's say it's a boy. Give me all the details. Make it up if you have to. I need juicy details to make up for my lack of a boyfriend." My cheeks heat and Danni doesn't miss it. "You're blushing. So there *is* a boy!" she squeals in excitement, clapping her hands together.

Groaning, I fold my arms on the table and drop

my head down onto them. "Yes, no...maybe. I don't know."

"Tell. Me. Everything."

I do—well the beginning, anyway, because the second she sees where I'm going, she stops me.

"Wait...please don't tell me you're fucking Ben. Oh my God, you are. You're fucking Ben. Ben, your stepbrother. Ben!"

"A little louder, please? The bartender in the staff room didn't quite hear you."

"Shit, fuck. I'm sorry. But fuck, Lauren. You're shagging your stepbrother? Do you have any idea how hot that is? Forbidden. But still, hot as fuck!"

I bite my tongue to stop myself agreeing.

Question after question falls from my best friend's mouth as she tries to piece together how I ended up sat here a broken mess.

"So is it over?"

"What? No. Well, I don't think so. I hope not." Panic at the thought alone crawls up my throat and I know that I'm in way too deep with this. No matter what happens next, this thing with Ben is going to shatter me.

"Maybe you'll get another nocturnal visit. He might sneak into your room, into your bed—"

"Stop, please," I beg, not needing the images in my head.

THE HOUSE IS in darkness when the taxi pulls up later that evening. It's way too late to be out on a school night, and I'm equally too pissed. It seems to be becoming a habit that I really need to get myself out of.

After shoving some money at the driver, I stagger my way towards the house. Leaning against the front door, I fumble with the key when it suddenly opens. As I fall forwards, I prepare for the pain that's surely going to follow, but instead of the solid stone floor, I hit a warm, hard, and very familiar body.

"Ben?" I ask, trying to get my eyes to focus so that I can see him.

"Where the fuck have you been?"

"Out," I snap, not liking the tone of his voice. It's too similar to Dad's—always demanding answers.

"Whoa, okay. I'm sorry," he soothes when I start fighting to get out of his arms. "It wasn't meant to come out like that. I was just worried when you weren't here and I couldn't get a hold of you."

"Sorry," I whisper, mortified that for even a moment I put him and my dad in the same box. "I just needed to get out of this house."

"Trust me, I understand that more than you could know."

He guides me towards the kitchen and, once he's happy I'm safe on the chair he's placed me on, he sets about getting me a glass of water and some tablets.

"I'm fine," I say when he hands them over.

"Now you are. In a few hours when you have to get ready for work, it's going to be another story."

Groaning, I swallow down the tablets.

Once he's cleared up any evidence we were here, Ben sweeps me up into his arms and carries me up the stairs.

"I can walk, you know."

"Sure you can, baby. I just love having you in my arms." I've no idea if the first part is meant to be sarcastic or not, but I let it go, enjoying the feeling of being pressed up against his hard body.

I don't realise I fall asleep in his arms, but the next thing I know I'm perched on the edge of my bed while Ben pulls my shirt over my head. Once my clothes are off, he stands and pulls his own t-shirt off before covering me with it. His scent surrounds me.

"Mmm, it smells like you," I mumble as he laughs at my drunken state.

"Strange, that. Do I need to get a bucket?" His words pass me by as I watch him take care of me. He's so kind and gentle with me that tears sting my eyes.

"I think I'm falling in love with you." It's not

until his face pales in front of me that I realise I said it out loud. "Shit," I whisper.

"No, Lauren. It's just the excitement, the thrill of being caught." He might be saying the words, but there's no strength behind them, and as I drift off, I wonder who he's trying to convince. Him or me?

CHAPTER ELEVEN

I FEEL like death when I wake up the next morning. It's not until I pry my eyes open that I realise it's not as bad as I first thought, because my head is resting on Ben's chest.

"Morning, baby. How are you feeling?" He laughs when I grunt and roll onto my back.

He goes to kiss me but must think better of it when I bite down on my lips. My mouth feels like the bottom of a bird's cage; I don't need to share it with anyone. His lips go to my neck instead, and almost immediately my hangover is put to one side.

"GOOD MORNING," Erica sings when she sees me walking into the office. "Did you have a good weekend? Wait, don't answer that...I can see it written all over your green face."

"I need tea," I mutter, walking past her desk and going straight to the kitchen.

"Sooo..." she purrs behind me. "Was it everything you thought it would be, even with the hangover from hell?"

I can't keep the smile from my face, and Erica squeals like a teenage girl. "It was...incredible. But the hangover is courtesy of my best friend. Dad and Jenny came home and things went to shit pretty quickly. I needed to get out and she was more than willing to ply me with cocktails if it meant she got the gossip."

"Sounds like a smart girl. Does your dad know?" Erica suddenly drops her voice and whispers the last bit.

"I'm still alive, aren't I?"

"Yeah, but the verdict's still out on Ben."

The memory of his hangover cure this morning makes my cheeks heat. "I'll take that blush as him still being alive, too...for now."

"I don't know what I'm going to do," I admit.

"I wish I had the answer for you, I really do. But in all honesty, I've no idea what advice to give you aside from enjoy yourself while you can."

My mood quickly depletes. The look Dad gives

me when he eventually appears from his office is one that would melt a weaker person, but I'm fed up with letting him run my life. I'm nearly nineteen, and it's about time he realised that his control-freak nature won't roll with me. Jenny might bend over backwards to make him happy, but I won't. It's bad enough I agreed to live with him, although I can't really regret that decision anymore because it brought me Ben.

I'm thoroughly pissed off when I march through the house later that evening. My hangover has long disappeared and I'm just about ready to start drinking all over again if it means forgetting my shitty day.

Aside from a tense few minutes in the kitchen with Dad and Jenny while I find myself some dinner, I hide out in my room, silently hoping I'll get a surprise visitor, but he never comes.

"LAUREN, GET IN HERE," Dad barks from his seat behind his desk.

"Sure thing, *boss,*" I mutter under my breath as I push my chair out and follow his demands.

"I need you to work late tonight."

"Great." The sarcasm in my voice causes his lips to press into a thin line.

"I need all the customer details from these," he says, pushing a massive stack of paper towards me. "Put into a spreadsheet."

"We've already got—"

"Are you questioning me?" he snaps, his eyes darkening with frustration.

"No. Whatever you need."

"What I need is for you to do your job without questioning everything. Can you do that?"

"Sure, but—"

"No buts, Lauren. Just go and do your damn job."

I walk out of his office with the stack of papers in my arms, tears stinging my eyes.

As I watch everyone else leave for the night, I'm still setting up the bloody spreadsheet Dad had drawn out for me on a scrap of paper. Spreadsheets are *not* my forte, so it takes much longer than it should.

I'm just making a start on inputting everything when the buzzer for the main door to the building rings out loud around the silent space around me. I glance at my phone, but I've got no messages or missed calls.

When it rings again, I make my way over and press the button to see who's at the door.

My heart turns over when I find Ben looking

back at me. "Are you going to let me in anytime soon?" he asks into the speaker.

"Yeah, sorry. Hang on." Pressing the button down, I give him time to enter the building before going over the office door to wait for him. "Mmm...this is a nice surprise," I say once he's released my lips.

"I got this really weird message from Mum telling me that she and your dad were going out to meet a client tonight and that you were working late. She never usually tells me shit like that—"

"She knows about us."

His eyes widen in panic. "She does?"

"I don't know for sure, but I've got a feeling."

"That would make sense," he says with a nod. "Anyway, I've come to help, and I've ordered pizza."

"My saviour," I sigh dramatically. "Surely you've got something better to do tonight than help me with this bullshit?"

"What are you doing?"

I walk over to my desk and explain.

"This is *bullshit*. This spreadsheet already exists." He clicks around in the server and pulls up a replica of what I'm creating.

"He just wanted me out of the house. I can't believe it." The frustration I was already feeling starts to morph into anger.

"I can."

"He's not going to get away with this." Grabbing my phone, I unlock it and go to call his number, but it's snatched from my hands.

"Think about this, Lauren. I'd love for you to call him up and rip him a new one, but do you want to make him any more suspicious than he already is? He thinks that, by giving you such a pointless task, he's keeping us apart. You can hardly tell him that I turned up to fuck you in his office and pointed this out."

I stare at him. The anger coursing through my veins suddenly turns into something else. "You came to fuck me on his desk?"

"Well, I came to help. I was just hopeful for more."

Stepping up to him, I press my lips to his. His hands start on my waist but are soon tangled in my hair as he deepens the kiss.

The buzzer going off again forces us to break apart. "I hope you like pizza."

"Who doesn't like pizza?"

He shrugs before walking over to the buzzer and letting the delivery guy in while I smooth my hair down.

"How did you know that spreadsheet exists?"

"I'm more involved in this business than everyone believes."

"Oh."

"This is my legacy. My future. I need to know that there's going to be something left for me when my time comes."

"Why wouldn't there be anything left? As far as I can see, the profits are only increasing year after year and our reputation is sky high."

"Things aren't always as they seem." It's not the first time he's said those words to me.

"So, what are they, then? What are you trying to say?"

He's silent for a few seconds as he tries to come up with an answer. "I don't want to drag you into it. Just be aware, is all."

Narrowing my eyes at him, I wait for him to elaborate, but it soon becomes clear that he's not going to say any more on the matter.

"Now, copy and paste that stuff into a new spreadsheet so it looks like you've made a start, and then meet me in your dad's office." He winks at me as he tidies up the pizza boxes and a rush of heat fills my body.

I shouldn't be fucking my stepbrother. I really shouldn't be fucking him on my dad's desk. And I really, *really* shouldn't be this excited about it.

I do what I need to do in case Dad starts asking questions first thing. I've no idea what Ben's doing, but I can hear him crashing about in Dad's office. My pulse thunders in my veins as I think about what's waiting for me on the other side of that door.

This is so very wrong, but I can't think of anything I want more right now.

By the time I hit save, my entire body is aching with anticipation for what's to come.

After shutting down the computer, I comb my fingers through my hair and wipe away any smudged makeup from under my eyes. It's crazy because he's been sitting here right next to me for the last hour, but I'm nervous.

My legs feel like jelly as I walk over to the door. I should just turn the handle and walk in, but something stops me.

With excitement and anticipation filling me, I lift my hand and gently knock the solid wood.

"Come in." His voice is deep and has tingles racing down my spine.

The door clicks as I turn the handle, then I push it open and walk in. I find Ben sitting in Dad's chair with his feet propped up on the edge of the desk like he owns the place.

If it wasn't for the pulsing muscle in his neck, I'd say he was totally unaffected by this situation, but I know it's not the case.

He's just as excited as I am right now.

"Strip," he demands. His fingers entwine across his stomach as he rests back in the chair like he's about to watch TV—only his sole focus in on my body.

My hands tremble a little as I lift them to the top button on my blouse, but I never move my eyes from his.

With each button I undo, his blue eyes darken and the muscle in his neck pulses faster. He's fighting to keep himself in that chair right now, and the knowledge that it's me causing that has fire burning in my belly and my confidence soaring.

Turning my back to him, I allow the fabric to fall from my shoulders and slowly drop down my arms, exposing my back. It flutters to the floor and I look over my shoulder just in time to watch him follow its journey.

When his attention comes back to me, his impatience is clear on his face. "More."

Nodding at his request, I unclip my bra. I make quick work of toeing off my shoes and unzipping and dropping my skirt, revealing my thong-clad arse to him. His groan of approval spurs me on.

"Fucking hell," he breathes when I turn. His eyes drop from mine in favour of my body. Heat burns a trail where his gaze roams my skin. My nipples pucker as if he's touching them and even more heat descends to my core.

"Come here. I want you on this desk."

Nerves find their way in when I notice a photo of Dad and Jenny on the sideboard, but knowing he's the sole reason I'm here working late in the first place helps me push the concern aside. As I walk past, I lie the frame face down so I don't have to look at them again.

There's just enough space between Ben and the desk, so after climbing over his leg, I settle myself with my arse on the edge.

Feeling brazen under his intense stare, I lift one leg at a time and place my foot on the armrest of the chair, exposing myself to him.

He swallows and shifts a little in his seat as he stares at the tiny bit of lace stopping him from seeing every part of me.

I rest back on my elbows, my chest heaving with my increased breaths, my breasts rising and falling at a rapid rate.

He rips his eyes from my centre and runs them up my body. My nipples tighten and my stomach clenches with the desire and need to be touched.

"What are you waiting for?" I moan. My voice doesn't even sound like my own.

"Just making sure I commit this to memory. I might need it one day."

His words darken the mood a little, but it's soon forgotten when he sits forward and reaches behind him to pull his t-shirt over his head.

He drops it to the floor before wrapping his fingers around the lace at my hips and pulling my thong down my legs. Lifting my arse to help him, coldness surrounds me until his warm breath replaces it.

I moan before his lips even touch me. Just the sensation of the stream of air he blows across me is enough to have me racing towards my release.

His tongue licks from my entrance all the way to my clit, my hips lift, and his arm rests across my lower stomach to keep me in place.

"Oh God, Ben," I moan as he teases around my clit and then lower, circling my entrance but never giving me quite what I need. "Please, please," I chant, threading my fingers in his hair and trying to force him deeper.

"All in good time, baby," he says, pulling away and wiping his mouth with the back of his hand.

Standing to full height, my eyes drop to his sculpted chest and then down to his waist when he starts undoing his jeans.

Biting down on my bottom lip, I impatiently wait for what I want, what I need.

He doesn't bother removing his jeans and boxers. Instead, he just pushes both down his thighs once he's pulled a condom from his pocket.

My muscles clench as I watch him rip the packet and roll it down his length. "Ben," I moan impatiently.

When he turns his eyes on me, they're dark, hungry, and possessive.

Everything about what we're doing right now is wrong, but it doesn't feel that way. What we're doing feels like the most natural thing in the world.

I whimper when he rubs the tip of his cock between my folds. I fall down onto the cold desk when he starts pushing inside me. The sensation takes over and I go limp as I enjoy everything he gives me.

My hips burn where his fingers grip tightly and the edge of the desk digs into my arse, but I don't care. I don't care about anything when he's touching me.

Needing more, his hands skim up my body. One tangles in my hair, lifting me from the desk to find his lips. His tongue invades my mouth and mimics what his cock's doing lower down in my body.

My hands run up his back before my nails

scratch all the way back down. He growls and, if it's possible, thrusts deeper inside me.

"Holy shit, Lauren," he groans when he pulls back from my lips. "Let me feel you. Let me feel you milking my cock."

"Oh God," I whimper as the first tingles of my orgasm erupt within me. "Oh God, Ben!" My body thrashes about in his arms as I give myself over to the pleasure. My head drops back as wave after wave rolls through me. It's only seconds until Ben swells inside me and I feel the first twitch of his release.

Ben pulls me tight against his chest, and we stay locked in our embrace as our heart rates decrease and our breathing slows.

I've no idea how much time passes, but eventually I pull my face from his neck and look up into his bright eyes. "So, was fucking me on Dad's desk everything you thought it'd be?"

He chuckles, and his semi-hard cock stirs inside me once again. "It was everything and more, baby."

THE REST of the week continues in a similar fashion, but I keep a closer eye on everything at work after Ben's words. I haven't seen or heard from him, and I miss him like crazy. By the time Friday rolls around, I'm receiving sympathetic looks from everyone in the office—bar Dad, of course. He seems totally unaware of my ever-souring mood as the hours pass by.

I'm just about ready to give up hope of seeing Ben tonight until I walk towards my bed. The sight of the Post-It note on my pillow has excitement racing through me. I forget about any frustration I have from not seeing enough of him and pluck it from its resting place.

I'll pick you up from the end of the street at 7pm. Wear something hot!

Glancing back at the clock, I see it's already gone six. I've got my work cut out for me if I'm going to be ready for a night out.

Rushing to my wardrobe, I thank God for the fact that I washed my favourite dress earlier in the week, and pull it from its hanger. I place my shoes next to it on my bed and rummage through my drawers to find the other set of lingerie I bought for the weekend but never wore.

I have the quickest shower of my life before standing in the mirror, trying to get my hair dry and my make-up applied in record time.

I'm flustered but ready by five-to-seven.

Grabbing my bag from the sideboard, I tuck my phone inside and go to leave the house.

"Lauren, you look beautiful. Hot date?" Jenny asks when I bump into her at the bottom of the stairs.

"J—just meeting a friend," I stutter. She hasn't said anything about us, but I've still got a nagging feeling that she knows what's going on. Maybe she's equally as scared of Dad's reaction if—when—he finds out.

"That sounds like fun. I'm home alone tonight," she says sadly. "Well, have a wonderful night."

"You, too." The second the words have passed my lips, I rush out of the house, not wanting to waste a second of my time with Ben.

I come to a stop at the end of the street when I hear the deep rumble of his engine pull up behind me.

"Hey, beautiful." The smile he gives me takes my breath away, and I realise just how much I've missed him.

My arse has barely touched the leather when his fingers slide into my hair and he pulls me over to his lips.

"Fucking missed you, baby." A deep ache forms in my lower stomach at his words.

"I thought maybe..."

"What?" he asks, staring deep into my eyes. I swear he can see every single one of my insecurities.

"That you'd changed your mind about us." It comes out as a whisper because, when he's looking at me the way he is right now, I know it's not true. I can see everything he feels for me—it's written all over his face. It's equally as terrifying as it is relieving.

"Never," he states. "You're mine, Lauren. You're not getting rid of me. No matter what happens, I'll always come back for you."

I didn't realise I wasn't breathing, but when he stops talking I release a long breath.

"Come on, let's get out of here."

"Where are we going?"

"It's a surprise."

Sitting back, I get comfortable for the drive. Ben's hand stays firmly attached to mine as we head towards our destination.

"So...where have you been?"

"Keeping my distance. But I've not been too far away." Glancing over, he winks at me.

"What?"

"You're a really heavy sleeper, aren't you?"

"I guess. Are you telling me you've been with me and I didn't know?"

"Might be," he chuckles. "Did you also know that you talk in your sleep?"

"Yeah, Mum used to tell me that. Did I say anything interesting?" The muscles in his neck tighten and his teeth clench. "Ben, what did I say?"

"Everything I needed to hear to know all of this is worth the risk."

"You're most definitely worth the risk." Lifting our joined hands, he presses a kiss to my knuckles.

"What is this place?" I ask as Ben pulls the car to a stop in front of an expensive-looking restaurant on the other side of the city.

"Somewhere I can treat you, knowing we're safe from prying eyes." My heart flips over at his thoughtfulness. After spending a weekend hidden inside the house and then the office, it'll be nice to have a normal night out with him without having to look over our shoulders in case we see anyone we know. "It's won a ton of awards for its food, so I thought it would be a good choice."

"I'd eat anything as long as it means I get to spend a night with you," I admit, but I instantly feel ridiculous at how cheesy it sounds.

"Stay there," he instructs, and I watch as he jumps from the car and races around to my side. I unbuckle myself as he pulls the door open and, the second he reaches in for me, I slide my hand into his and allow him to pull me from the car. His actions are so far from the Ben I used to know—the angry, brooding teenager who hated the world around him. The man in front of me is all gentleman.

He pulls me up so I'm pressed against his chest. His breath tickles my ear as he leans in. "I think that might be the nicest thing anyone's ever said to me."

It takes me a moment to recall what I said, and I can't help laugh when I do. That is, until I realise he's not laughing with me. Lifting my head, I'm surprised by the serious look on his face. Shit, he's not joking.

"Ben, I—"

"Stop." I'm forced to do as he says when his fingers land on my lips. "Let's not go there. Tonight is about enjoying ourselves, not worrying about reality." Taking my hand, he leads me inside the restaurant.

It's exactly as I imagined it would be. The lighting is soft and candles flicker from the centre of the tables. There are a handful of couples enjoying their meals together, and mellow music fills the space. It is by far the most lavish and romantic restaurant I've ever stepped foot in. I feel totally out of place.

"What's wrong?" Ben asks when I don't immediately fall into place behind him and the maître d'.

"It's just so fancy."

"It's no less than you deserve." Looking at all the mature couples dining around us, I feel every bit my eighteen years and totally in over my head. "We can go somewhere else if you'd feel more comfortable."

"No. I'm just being silly. This will be amazing." I feel ridiculous making a fuss after he's gone to the effort of organising it. The second I saw him wearing a white dress shirt and trousers I knew I'd made the right choice with my dress, but never in a million years was I expecting something like this.

We're seated in a cosy corner of the room, and we order our drinks. It feels like no sooner has the waiter left, then he's back, placing glasses down in front of both of us and reeling off tonight's specials. I try my best to focus, but other than remembering that one involves chicken and another fish, I've no clue what they are. I'm still too stunned with how my Friday night is shaping up.

"I feel way too young for this," I whisper to Ben.

"Age is only a number. You couldn't look more at home, or any more beautiful." Sliding my chair over so that it's closer to his, he leans in and places a kiss at the corner of my lips. "I've been waiting all week for this."

"Me, too, I just didn't know it was coming."

Sadness washes through him once again but he doesn't say anything.

"What's the matter?" I prompt, hoping he'll open up.

"I hate this. I hate having to hide. I hate having to treat you like a dirty little secret."

"Me, too. But there's not much else we can do."

"How drunk were you on Sunday night?"

"Uh..." I stutter, a little shocked by his sudden topic change. "Pretty drunk, why?"

"Drunk enough to not remember what you said to me?"

I run what I can remember of that night through my head. I almost say that I don't remember, until something hits me. *Fuck, did I say that out loud? Did I really tell him I was falling in love with him?* I don't need to say any more. He sees the moment the realisation hits.

"Did you mean it, or was it the drink talking?" Casting my gaze over his shoulder, I try to figure out how to vocalise my feelings. "Don't hide from me," he demands softly, his fingers touching my cheek and bringing my eyes back to his. The hope in his eyes is enough to pull an honest answer out of me.

"Yes. I meant every word."

His eyes flash with emotion before he nods like he's made some big decision. I go to ask, but he beats me to it. "I'm going to talk to your dad."

"You're going to what? You can't. He'll...he'll..."

"He'll what? Really, what's he going to do? We're

both adults. He can't really stop us from seeing each other. Technically, we're not doing anything wrong."

My heart races and my hands tremble with the force of the sheer panic that rushes through me. I've witnessed arguments between Dad and Ben, and they're not pretty at the best of times. I can only imagine what will happen if he does this.

"No, it should come from me."

Ben's face hardens. "No. I won't let you do that."

"What? Why?"

"I don't trust him."

"What are you talking about? I'm his daughter, he won't do anything to me. It's safer coming from me. I might be able to calm him down about it."

"I doubt that very much. He's going to lose his shit."

"Then we won't tell him yet. Let's just enjoy ourselves."

Ben's face twists with uncertainty, and I know exactly how he feels. This fight between what we want and what we know is right is exhausting. "It'll be worse if he finds out before we tell him."

"Then we just have to be really careful." I can tell he's not happy about it. Neither am I, but there's no way I'm giving up on us.

Leaning into my ear, he whispers, "You'll have to stop screaming my name so loud."

My face is burning red when the waiter comes over with our starters. Ben just sits and chuckles at me. It's infectious as well as a relief to move on from our serious conversation. As much as it warms my heart that he seems to be thinking about a future for us, it also fills me with dread because I know that, as much as we might want to be together, doing so is going to involve a lot of pain.

I'M aware of new diners coming and going but I'm too consumed with the man beside me and the incredible food we're being served to take too much notice. That is, until a shiver runs down my spine. Untangling my fingers from Ben's across the table, I look up, but the ball of dread that's formed in my belly already knows what—or rather, who—I'm about to find.

I try to swallow down my panic as I look up into the angry eyes of my father with another woman on his arm. But he's not focused on me. His death stare is on the person next to me, who is currently totally unaware of the situation unfolding in front of him.

"Ben," I whisper, not taking my eyes from my dad for a second for fear of what he might do.

"Yeah, baby? What's—" His stare follows mine

until he finds the reason for my concern. "It'll be fine." I'm sure he's trying to reassure me, but it's not working.

Silence descends as the tension grows. Dad's anger is palpable, and I start to think he's going to fly at Ben at any second.

"Nick, this is a surprise. I bet Mum loves this place. Oh, you don't seem to have brought her."

"What the fuck are you doing?" I whisper through gritted teeth. Surely, pointing out that he's here with a woman who isn't my stepmum is not the thing to say right now. Ben ignores me, instead continuing his stare-off with my dad while the waiter stands with his eyes flicking between the two of them, not knowing what the hell is going on.

"What I'm doing isn't any of your concern, boy. Unfortunately for you, what *you* are doing seems to have everything to do with me. Care to explain what you're doing here with my daughter?"

"We're—" Ben starts, but Dad's having none of it. Marching forward, he lifts Ben from his seat and pushes him back until he's up against the wall.

"What the fuck are you doing with her?" Dad growls in Ben's face. "If you've fucking touched her..."

Every person in the restaurant turns to take in

the evening's entertainment, and my own anger bubbles over.

"Get off him." I pull at the arm holding Ben up against the wall. I've no doubt that Ben could overpower him, yet he just stands there.

"Lauren, go home," Dad demands, and it only adds fuel to my fire.

"Not a fucking chance. Get your hands off him. He wasn't doing anything wrong."

"I warned him what would happen if he so much as touched you."

"Dad, please." The waiter flits about behind me, clearly not used to this kind of situation, and I try to come up with something. "I love him."

"You *what?*" It's the first time Dad looks at me. When our eyes connect, fear races through me.

Letting go of Ben, he steps back like he's been winded. I breathe a sigh of relief that it's over, but I soon realise it's only the start. Dad pulls his fist back, his eyes locked on Ben, who's still staring at me.

"No!" I shriek, running to get between them. I'm too slow. Dad's already committed to throwing the punch, only instead of landing on the person he was intending to hit, it connects with my cheek.

"You motherfucker!" Ben roars, pushing himself off the wall and forcefully shoving my Dad out of the way so he can get to me. Unfortunately, Dad's so pumped up that he ignores me, still clutching my face while on the floor, and he goes for Ben. The noise that comes from Dad's throat is something I'd expect to hear from an animal, not a human—and certainly not my fucking father.

"I've called the police," someone shouts, and my Dad stops.

Blood drips from Ben's lip and his eye swells, but he doesn't cower away from Dad. "This whole restaurant just witnessed you assaulting both me and your own daughter. I suggest you get the hell out of here," he spits. "And take that cheap slut with you." His lip curls in disgust as he glances at the woman over Dad's shoulder.

"This isn't over," he warns. "Lauren, come on."

"No fucking way. I'm not letting you anywhere near her." The two of them stare at each other until the sound of sirens filters through the restaurant. Dad turns on his heel and marches towards the door, the woman hot on his heels.

"Fucking hell, are you okay?" Ben drops to his knees beside me and gently takes my face in his hands. His eyes run over every inch of my face, looking for injuries. His hands tremble, making the tears in my eyes finally drop. "Fuck."

His thumbs wipe the moisture away and I'm lifted into his arms. Somehow, he manages to pull out a wad of cash from his pocket and, after apologising to the poor waiter who's still standing there looking shell-shocked, he carries me from the restaurant.

The police car comes to a stop outside just as Ben pulls away from the curb. "Shouldn't we have stayed to speak to them?"

"Do you think sending the cops after your dad is going to make this any better?"

"No, probably not. I'm so sorry, I—"

"Lauren, none of this is your fault. You have nothing to apologise for."

"But your face."

"Trust me, it's looked a hell of a lot worse. He's right about one thing, though. I never should have touched you. You're way too good for an arsehole like me. I deserved a solid punch for that."

"Stop talking about yourself like that." He quickly glances over at me and my heart breaks at the look on his face. "I meant it, Ben. I love you."

His grip on the wheel tightens, turning his knuckles white. He blows out a long breath and stares ahead. I can't help feeling like my words just hurt more than my dad's fists, but I've no clue why.

"Stay here," he demands, pulling up in front of a shop. I have little choice but to do as he says, so I sit in the dark and wait. My phone vibrates in my bag but I don't have the energy to find out who it is. It's probably Dad ready to fire some more fucks into me for my stupid actions. Rolling my eyes at his childish behaviour, I rest my head back and close my eyes. My cheek throbs and ruins any chance I might have had of forgetting the last hour of my life.

My mind replays this evening over and over, trying to figure out how it all went so wrong. What were the chances of him being in the same restaurant on the other side of London? The shock I saw on his face when I first looked up, before his anger took over, told me that he hadn't followed us.

It really was just a horrific coincidence.

The image of the red-headed woman standing behind him pops up, and I feel like I'm going to puke. I didn't believe Ben all those weeks ago when he first found me in their kitchen and accused me of being my dad's bit on the side. I was aware it was his wandering ways that broke him and Mum up, but I really thought he was serious about Jenny. Knowing the only reason he was in that restaurant in the first place was because he was also hiding a dirty secret ensures that my stomach continues to turn over. I guess it gives us some ammunition when we go home and confront him about all of this.

"Don't fall asleep," Ben says the second he pulls the door open.

"I wasn't."

"You might have a concussion."

"I'm fine. Honestly. I didn't hit my head."

Dropping a couple of bags at my feet, he starts the car and pulls away from the curb. Silence descends around us. I hate the uncertainty I'm suddenly feeling. I knew Dad finding out was going to change things, but I wasn't expecting what happened.

"A hotel?" I ask when Ben pulls up into the underground car park.

"What? You wanted to go home?" The laugh that falls from him holds no amusement.

"No. I'd quite happily never go back there again."

"Now you understand a little of how I feel about that place." He throws both our phones in the glove compartment after turning off the engine, and I couldn't be happier to be cut off from the rest of the world after everything that's happened tonight.

With my hand locked in his, we walk towards the entrance and book a room. The woman's face behind reception twists in concern the moment she sees the state of us, but she soon drags her gaze away and hands over a key.

Knowing that we're going to be able to at least enjoy the rest of our night together before we face reality does have me breathing a little easier, although it doesn't mean I forget everything we've got coming our way when we do eventually go home.

"Go lie down." Ben pushes me towards the bed, then goes into the bathroom briefly with the bags. I listen as he runs the tap before he reappears with a glass of water, a packet of painkillers, and a bag of frozen peas. "Here, take these."

"I really am fine. You're the one who needs taking care of." I wince as he presses the cold peas to my cheek. "Please, let me look after you."

Placing my hand over his, I look up into his eyes, pleading with him.

"Fine," he whispers. "But be warned, I'm not used to being looked after."

Getting up from the bed, I go in search of something to clean up his face with. I dampen some tissue with warm water and head back into the bedroom. I find Ben still sat where I left him on the edge of the bed.

I unfasten his shirt buttons and push the fabric from his shoulders. He watches me through sad, swollen eyes.

"Scoot back." He does as I say, and in seconds he's resting back against the headboard.

I pull my dress up my thighs and throw my leg over him. After running my eyes over his face, I press some tissue to his blood-stained chin and attempt to clean him up. He winces when I brush past the cut, but he allows me to continue.

"I'm so sorry for—"

"Stop apologising for him. His actions have nothing to do with you."

"I know. But—"

"No. No buts. I'll always fight for you, Lauren, whether that's with your dad or anyone else who disapproves of this." His hips flex and I feel his length against me. Warm fingers wrap around my wrist, stopping me. He plucks the tissue from my fingers and drops it to the bed before pulling me down to him. "Me and you, Lauren. I'll always fight for you...protect you. Always."

His hands push my dress higher up my thighs and fingers slip inside my knickers.

"Always so wet for me," he murmurs as he finds my clit.

Groaning in pleasure, I grind myself on his fingers. I need the release that only he can give me after the night we've had. He works me into a frenzy before pulling his fingers out of me and undoing his trousers.

"Pocket," he grunts, and I dig around until I find the condom.

He goes to take it from my fingers but I hold tight. "Can I?"

His eyes darken with desire. "Be my guest."

I help him free himself and push the fabric down his thighs before I roll the condom down over his length.

"Over to you, then, baby."

Lifting myself up, I pull my knickers to the side and slide down onto him. We both sigh in pleasure.

"I'll never get enough of this." His hands come up and squeeze my breasts, and it only makes my impending orgasm build faster.

All of the stress from tonight falls away as I focus on the sensations that fill my body. I keep my movements slow, enjoying the feeling of him filling me to the hilt.

Circling my hips when I'm fully seated, I gasp when he hits me so deep that it almost sends me spiralling into my release.

"Let go, baby. That's it." His eyes stay locked on mine, his hands on my hips, helping me move.

Rotating my hips once more, light explodes behind my eyes and my body twitches and pulsates around him. I fight to keep my eyes on his but I lose the battle, the pleasure surging through me too violently.

Falling down onto his chest, I'm vaguely aware of him thrusting up into me until he groans and stills before his cock twitches, releasing everything he has.

His hands run up and down my back. It's relaxing, but reality soon starts to creep back in.

I reach for the bag of frozen peas still on the bed. Lifting them takes all my energy, but I manage to press them against Ben's eye.

"It's fine." He tries to move them away but I'm not having it. I feel pretty useless right now, and this is the only thing I can think of that will hopefully make somewhat of a difference.

The rest of the night is mostly filled with silence. We're both too lost in our own thoughts—or nightmares—to want to chat much. When I discover the bath has a Jacuzzi, I get it going and fill it with the salts I find on the side.

Even with the warmth of the water and the relaxing scent filling the room, Ben's muscles are still pulled tight. I can only imagine how he's feeling.

"I can't stop seeing him hitting you," he whispers once we're curled up in bed. He pulls me even tighter to him. "Every time I close my eyes, his fist is flying to your face. No man should ever hit a woman. *Ever*."

"I was trying to stop him from hitting you. He didn't mean to hit me," I argue, but I know it's weak at best.

"It doesn't matter. He still hit you. I was meant to

be protecting you. I *promised* I'd protect you, and yet that arsehole hit you. In front of me."

Running my hand up his chest, I wrap my fingers around his neck and make him look at me.

"None of what happened tonight was your fault, Ben. You need to stop blaming yourself. There was nothing you could have done."

"I never should have allowed myself to touch you. Your dad's right. I'm bad news."

"Shut up, right now. Do not believe a word that comes from his mouth. He doesn't know you. You're incredible, Ben."

He makes an unintelligible noise and tries to push me away.

"No. I won't let you do this. I won't let you pull away from me." Wrapping my arm around his waist and throwing my leg over his, I hold him as tightly as I possibly can. No more words are said between us—we're too lost in our own heads—but eventually we must drift off to sleep in each other's arms.

CHAPTER TWELVE

NO WORDS NEED to be exchanged the next morning. Just one look at each other and we know everything's about to change. I can't imagine a situation where Dad allows us to be together, but I'm not letting Ben go. Screw the business and the education I've been promised.

Other things in life are more important.

"I'm not ready," I admit when Ben comes back from the bathroom and begins pulling his clothes on.

"What's the point in putting off the inevitable? We need to go and face the music."

"Just a little longer?" I plead, hoping to live in this little bubble we've created for just a few more hours.

"We'll have lunch, then we're going back." If I

couldn't see Ben's face, I would think the words he's saying aren't affecting him. He seems so strong and sure of what we've got to do, but in reality, I can feel the fear the uncertainty radiating off him. It breaks my heart to know he's hurting because of my dad again. But what can I do?

I stand to the side while Ben hands the key over to the receptionist, fighting to keep in the tears stinging my eyes. I just want to curl up in a ball and cry. Through hazy eyes, I take him in, head to toe. I'm not ready for this to be over yet. We've got so much more to get to know about each other. We deserve more time.

His eyes widen when he turns and finds me staring at him, but he doesn't say anything. Nothing he can say can make this any better.

I get a bit of déjà vu when he pulls up in front of the same shop we stopped at last night and tells me to stay put.

I will my brain to stop, but it continues to race. It feels like no time has passed at all when he pulls the door open and climbs back in. The more I pray for our time together to last just a little bit longer, the faster it seems to go.

I expect him to take us to a café or restaurant for lunch, so I'm a little surprised when he pulls up in the same car park he brought me the first day we really spent any time together. That day feels like a million years ago, now.

"This is where it all started," he says sadly. "It seemed like a perfect place to—"

"Do not finish that sentence." If he says the words I fear are coming, I'm going to lose it. Instead he nods, grabs the bag of food he bought, and climbs out of the car. His shoulders hang like he's got the weight of the world on them. With a sigh, I follow his lead.

After retrieving a blanket from the boot, we walk hand in hand over to the oak tree and set up our little picnic. The sun might be shining, but it feels like we've got a giant black rain cloud hanging over us, and I realise that as much as I want to put off going home, right now is torture. Looking at Ben, knowing this could be the end is just too much to bear.

"Fancy a sausage roll?" A weak laugh passes my lips at his attempt at a joke. "Lauren, you need to eat something."

"I can't. I feel sick."

I expect him to argue, but once again he just nods.

"I GUESS we should get this over with, then?" I ask after we've been sitting on the blanket in silence for well over an hour.

"Just one more thing." Crawling over to me, Ben cups the back of my head and gently lowers me down. His lips tickle against mine and I just about manage to hold back a sob.

His kiss is so gentle and so full of emotion. My heart pounds like it's going to explode out of my chest. For some reason, this kiss feels final, like it could be a goodbye, and it has a lump forming in my throat at just the thought of this being the end for us.

Turning my head from his lips, my first tear falls.

"Lauren," he whispers, running his nose across my cheek until his lips are at my ears. "I love you, too."

The sob I was holding in erupts. I want to scream. I want to shout about the unfairness of all this, but I know it won't help. Even if Dad were to hear it, it wouldn't make one ounce of difference.

Silence hangs heavy between us during the drive home. Our phones continue to vibrate from where we stashed them in the glove box yesterday and it's just another reminder of what's waiting for us.

I'm surprised when Ben pulls into the driveway to find only my car parked in front of the house. I expected the most depressing welcome home party ever.

Reaching over, Ben pulls both phones from their hiding place and hands mine over before unlocking his and reading through messages. I don't bother looking. I've got plenty of time for that later.

"Come on. I really need to get out of these clothes."

I can only agree—we're both still wearing the outfits we chose for our meal last night.

No one's home and the house seems creepier than ever as we walk through it. I feel like I'm being watched, but as I look over my shoulder, it's only Ben who follows me up the stairs.

Every time I hear a noise, my heart jumps in my throat, thinking he's going to come barrelling through the door. But he never does. When a key does slide in the lock while we're on the sofa trying to watch TV, it's Jenny who appears in the doorway, looking her usual self. She's does a double take when she sees Ben's black eye and cut lip, but she doesn't ask. I know for a fact it's not the first time he's come home after fighting. After asking us if we're okay, she turns to leave.

"Where's Dad?" I ask before she disappears.

"A golf weekend with a client, sweetheart. He won't be back until tomorrow."

Ben's eyes burn into the back of my head, and when I turn around, he mouths, *Golf weekend?*

Shaking my head, I stand. I need to do something or I'm going to go stir-crazy waiting for him to appear.

"What are you doing?" Ben asks in a panic when I go to leave the room.

"Going for a walk."

"Wait. I'll come."

"No." He looks totally taken aback by my refusal, but I just need a few minutes to myself. "I just need—"

"It's okay. I get it. I'll be here when you get back."

"Promise?"

"Of course."

Sliding on a pair of trainers, I leave the house and head off down the street. I've no route in mind. All I know is that I need to move. Pulling my phone from my pocket, I look down at all the notifications. To my surprise, almost all of them are from Mum. Ignoring the missed calls and voicemails, I open my messages.

> Mum: Your dad just called. Are you okay?

> Mum: Honey, please just let me know you're safe.

> Mum: Lauren. I'm worried. Ring me back.

There's a whole stream of messages from her, and I feel awful that she's been dragged into this, and even worse that I've given her a reason to worry.

"Lauren, are you okay?" she asks in a rush the second she answers the phone.

"Yes, I'm fine. I'm so sorry. We left our phones in the car. If I knew he'd called you I never would have—"

"It's okay, as long as you're okay."

"I am." I ignore the throbbing that comes from the purple bruise on my temple. Bringing that up would only anger her more.

"What the hell happened?"

I recount everything from the night before, much to her horror, although I omit the bit about Dad's fist colliding with my head and focus on him attacking Ben.

"Don't say I didn't warn you, honey."

"I know, I know. It was inevitable. It's just what happens next that I'm freaking out about. If he's capable of doing that in the middle of a busy restaurant, what's he going to do in the solitude of his own home?" I hate to say the words aloud, but I'm scared for Ben. Something tells me that what we experienced last night was only the tip of the iceberg.

"It might not be as bad as you think." She's trying

to be supportive, but I can hear the quiver in her voice loud and clear. "Now that he's had time to calm down, he might see things a little differently."

I have to bite down on my lip to stop myself from asking if she's joking or not.

By the time I walk back up the driveway, the sun's starting to set. Ben rushes from the kitchen, looking harassed as I toe my shoes off.

"Fucking hell, Lauren." The second he's in reaching distance, he pulls me into him. I stiffen the second I'm in his arms, aware that we're standing in the middle of the hallway for anyone to see. "It's okay. He's not here." His words do little to relax me.

No, he's not here right now.

But he's coming.

For the first time since I moved in, we spend the evening like a normal family. Jenny cooks and the three of us sit around the table, chatting. It's weirdly enjoyable, even with the huge elephant in the corner of the room. She shows no sign of knowing anything about us or last night, so I can only assume she really believes that Dad's on a golfing weekend and not banging the red-head from the restaurant. I feel for her, but my sympathy only goes so far because I've got enough of my own problems to worry about.

Once we've all cleaned up, we make our excuses

and disappear off in different directions. I head up to my room, hoping that in a few minutes Ben will follow. I'm not disappointed. We spend the whole night on my bed watching crappy Saturday night quiz shows and continuing to ignore the inevitable.

After hearing Jenny come up to bed, Ben turns the TV up a couple of notches and sets about making me scream, albeit quietly.

I'm sure it's just everything fucking up my head, but I swear there's something different about him when he slides into me. His eyes lock with mine and it's like he's trying to tell me something that he's not brave enough to say out loud. It makes my heart constrict and I have to remind myself that he's here.

And I just pray that everything's going to be okay.

We fall asleep wrapped in each other's arms, just as it should be, but I can't shift the feeling that something's very wrong.

I wake up a couple of times in the night and snuggle tighter against Ben's warm body, knowing that as long as he's here with me, everything's going to be okay.

I WAKE WITH A START. Sitting up, my heart races from a nightmare that seemed so real only moments ago. The image of Ben's back as he walked away from me is burned into my mind. The look in his eyes that screamed that he didn't want this but had no choice has a lump growing in my throat.

Reaching out, I expect to find him sleeping next to me but all I find is a cold, empty bed. When I turn to look, dread settles in my stomach. *That was just a nightmare, right?* I soon get my answer though, when I find a Post-It note on his pillow.

I promised to protect you, and this is the only way I know how.
Forever yours, Ben x

A tear splashes against the paper, making the ink run.

No, no, no.

This must be a joke. My heart thunders in my chest as I drop the note and scramble from my bed. Pulling on one of his t-shirts, I open my door and race towards his.

I tell myself that he's going to be there. He'll just be in the shower and this is all one very bad dream. But as I push the door open, I'm greeted with silence and I know it's wishful thinking. All his stuff might still be here, but I know the truth.

I feel it in my heart.

He's gone.

Falling down on his bed, I pull his pillow to me and cry. I cry for what we had as well as for what we've both lost.

I've no idea how long I'm there for, but when I hear movement downstairs and a deep male voice, I know it's time to find out everything. The real truth. Wiping my swollen and sore eyes, I pull my hair away from my face and secure it in a bun with the band around my wrist, preparing to fight.

"What the hell did you do?" I roar as I run down the last few steps, seeing my dad putting his overnight bag down in the hallway. "What did you do?" I fly at him, my arms taking on a life of their own as I try to slap and punch him. My heart breaks all over again and tears stream down my cheeks. His arms come up to protect his face as I hear Jenny's footsteps behind me.

"Lauren, what on earth?" Her arms wrap around my waist, but she's too weak and I fight her off in my need to get to him.

To *hurt* him. I need to do something that's going to take away the agonising pain of my heart splitting in two.

My arms start to burn as I fight to drag in air between my wailing, and he must see I start to tire because he reaches out and wraps his fingers around my wrists to stop me.

"What the hell is wrong with you?"

"You. You are what's wrong with me," I seethe, staring up into his hard, cold eyes. "What did you do? What did you say to him?" My body's limp, exhausted, and drained from the emotion that's washed through it in the past few minutes.

"Lauren, I've no clue what you're talking about?"

"He's gone, Dad. Gone. I know it's because of you." All I feel is emptiness as I say those words out loud.

"Who's gone?" Jenny asks, but I can already tell by the flat tone of her voice that she knows.

"Ben. He's gone, and it's all his fault." I thrash to get out of his hold and this time he lets me go.

"Where's he gone?"

"I don't fucking know. But this arsehole here sent him away."

"Lauren," he warns, but I cut him off when he starts to say more.

"Don't even think of chastising me for my language because you deserve much, much worse. Were you not content with controlling my education and career? You also had to weigh in on my love life? You're a fucking joke as a father. A *fucking* joke."

"Enough!" he roars. His fists clench and I flinch away from him, afraid to be on the wrong end of them again. "I haven't done anything. I've been at golf all weekend. I—"

"You're a fucking liar," I scream.

"I went to golf *after* my business meeting on Friday night."

A laugh falls from my lips, but it's anything but amused. "Golf? Was that her name? There's no way he'd have left by choice. *You* sent him away."

"Trust me, Lauren. I wish I got the chance. I'd have done it years ago if I could." I don't miss Jenny's gasp behind me, but we both ignore her. "He's a fucking waste of space. Nothing but bad news. You're better off as far away from him as you can get. This just proves what kind of man he really is, don't you think? He's been caught out and he's run. All he was trying to do was piss me off, trying to show that he's better than me by doing something I forbade him to. I told him very specifically what I would do to him if he came anywhere near you, but he did it anyway. Now, he's running scared. You don't deserve someone like him, Lauren. You deserve a real man, someone who'll stand by you and fight for you. Not a pussy like him."

"No, no. You're lying. He wouldn't just leave. I don't believe you."

"I swear to you, Lauren. I haven't done anything. I was expecting to come home now to sort this whole mess out."

"This isn't a mess, Dad." I shout, shoving my palms at his chest. "It's my life and you're fucking ruining it. You're ruining everything."

"I haven't—"

"You're a fucking liar. You don't care about me and what I do. All you care about it keeping up appearances and making money. You don't care about me," I repeat. The reality of the situation hits me. Fresh tears spill from my eyes, my fight draining from my body.

"Of course I care. I only want the best for you, Lauren. What's he's done just proves he's not good enough for you. He should be standing here now fighting for you."

"No, he wouldn't just leave me. He wouldn't. What we have...it's...it's..."

Dad's face softens, and for the first time since he walked through the door, I see concern on his face. "I'm sorry you're hurting. Come here, sweetheart."

I'm too weak to do anything but what he suggests, and I fall into his arms. He holds me as I cry and rubs my back to try to calm me. I was so convinced that this was his doing. I never even considered that Ben didn't want this as much as I did. I took all his words as gospel, and it's only now that I doubt everything he ever said to me.

Dad guides me into the living room, stopping to kiss Jenny on the cheek as we move past her. "It's for the best," he says, but I don't know if he's talking to her or me.

EVERYTHING CONTINUES around me like my world hasn't shifted on its axis. The house feels even colder than it used to. Even the office feels different without his presence. Everything I used to enjoy or look forward to just seems dull. Or maybe it's just me who's dull and lifeless. The hurt won't leave. No matter what I try to do to distract myself, he's always there in my heart. It's just a constant reminder of what I thought I'd found.

It's been a month since Ben walked out of my life, but I still can't seem to pull myself out of the hole I've fallen into. My heart aches more with every day that passes, and my anger at him grows. After everything, how could he just walk away like I meant nothing to him?

His bedroom door stays closed, and I have to fight

not to look at it every time I walk past. Dad and Jenny have both been incredible and allowed me the time I need to attempt to put myself back together, but I fear that I'm never going to be the same again. Even with them in the same house, I'm lonely. I'm lonelier than I've ever experienced despite everyone doing their best to distract me.

They say it's better to have loved and lost than to have never loved at all, but right now I call bullshit, because I'm pretty sure I'd take never meeting him over the daily agony of this broken heart.

Ben Johnson was my first love.

My first everything.

I'll never forget everything he gave me.

And I'll never forgive him for taking it all away.

***

Ben and Lauren's story continues in *Losing the Forbidden* DOWNLOAD NOW

WHAT TO KNOW where it all began? Ben originally appeared as a secondary character in my

Falling series and totally stole my heart. While you're waiting for *Losing for Forbidden* to release you can get started with *Falling for Ryan*.

DOWNLOAD NOW

ACKNOWLEDGMENTS

Nothing about this book has really gone as planned. Knowing BJ, I guess I shouldn't be surprised. This first part of his and Lauren's story was meant to be short, but as I delved deeper and deeper into the beginning of their relationship, I just couldn't stop.

I've loved Ben since I first mentioned his character—in *Falling For Lucas*, I think. As I wrote each following book, it just became more and more obvious to me that he'd have to have his own story. He likes to make out that he's just a player and happy to have a revolving door on his bedroom, but he's keeping a lot hidden. Mostly his heart, as you've seen.

I really hope you enjoyed this first instalment of their story. I'm seriously excited to discover where they're going to take me next.

As far as thank-yous go, as always I need to start with Michelle, for alpha reading this as I typed it and putting up with the nonsense that comes from my fingertips. It's a good job we're mostly on the same wavelength or she'd have no idea what I was trying to say.

My betas, Deanna, Helen, Lindsay, Suzanne and Tracy. Where would I be without you? Thank you so much for all your honest feedback and your love of my characters and books.

Evelyn, once again, for digging your way through a million typos to make this book as good as it possibly can be. I'd be nowhere without you.

Michelle, thank you for proofreading for me once again. You must be getting bored of the amount of words of mine you've read recently!

And finally, my husband and daughter for supporting me through this journey, pushing me forward and inspiring me every day.

Until next time,

Tracy xo

ABOUT THE AUTHOR

Tracy Lorraine is a *USA Today* and *Wall Street Journal* bestselling new adult and contemporary romance author. Tracy has recently turned thirty and lives in a cute Cotswold village in England with her husband, baby girl and lovable but slightly crazy dog. Having always been a bookaholic with her head stuck in her Kindle, Tracy decided to try her hand at a story idea she dreamt up and hasn't looked back since.

Be the first to find out about new releases and offers. Sign up to my newsletter here.

If you want to know what I'm up to and see teasers and snippets of what I'm working on, then you need to be in my Facebook group. Join Tracy's Angels here.

Keep up to date with Tracy's books at
www.tracylorraine.com

Falling Series

Falling for Ryan: Part One #1

Falling for Ryan: Part Two #2

Falling for Jax #3

Falling for Daniel (A Falling Series Novella)

Falling for Ruben #4

Falling for Fin #5

Falling for Lucas #6

Falling for Caleb #7

Falling for Declan #8

Falling For Liam #9

Forbidden Series

Falling for the Forbidden #1

Losing the Forbidden #2

Fighting for the Forbidden #3

Craving Redemption #4

Demanding Redemption #5

Avoiding Temptation #6

<u>Chasing Temptation</u> #7

<u>Rebel Ink Series</u>

<u>Hate You</u> #1

<u>Trick You</u> #2

<u>Defy You</u> #3

<u>Play You</u> #4

<u>Inked</u> (A Rebel Ink/Driven Crossover)

<u>Rosewood High Series</u>

<u>Thorn</u> #1

<u>Paine</u> #2

<u>Savage</u> #3

<u>Fierce</u> #4

<u>Hunter</u> #5

Faze (#6 Prequel)

<u>Fury</u> #6

<u>Legend</u> #7

<u>Maddison Kings University Series</u>

<u>TMYM: Prequel</u>

<u>TRYS</u> #1

<u>TDYW</u> #2

<u>TBYS</u> #3

<u>TVYC</u> #4

<u>TDYD</u> #5

<u>TDYR</u> #6

<u>TRYD</u> #7

<u>Knight's Ridge Empire Series</u>

<u>Wicked Summer Knight</u>: Prequel (Stella & Seb)

<u>Wicked Knight</u> #1 (Stella & Seb)

<u>Wicked Princess</u> #2 (Stella & Seb)

<u>Wicked Empire</u> #3 (Stella & Seb)

<u>Deviant Knight</u> #4 (Emmie & Theo)

<u>Deviant Princess</u> #5 (Emmie & Theo

<u>Deviant Reign</u> #6 (Emmie & Theo)

<u>One Reckless Knight</u> (Jodie & Toby)

<u>Reckless Knight</u> #7 (Jodie & Toby)

<u>Reckless Princess</u> #8 (Jodie & Toby)

<u>Reckless Dynasty</u> #9 (Jodie & Toby)

<u>Dark Halloween Knight</u> (Calli & Batman)

<u>Dark Knight</u> #10 (Calli & Batman)

<u>Dark Princess</u> #11 (Calli & Batman)

Dark Legacy #12 (Calli & Batman)

Corrupt Valentine Knight (Nico & Siren)

Ruined Series

Ruined Plans #1

Ruined by Lies #2

Ruined Promises #3

Never Forget Series

Never Forget Him #1

Never Forget Us #2

Everywhere & Nowhere #3

Chasing Series

Chasing Logan

The Cocktail Girls

His Manhattan

Her Kensington

Falling for the Forbidden is a spin off from my *Falling* series. If you've not read it then keep reading for a sneak peek at *Falling for Ryan*, my friends to lovers romance that kicks off the series.

FALLING FOR RYAN: PART ONE

Molly

Eight years ago...

"MUM, I'm going to Becky's sixteenth birthday party tonight, then sleeping at Hannah's," I remind her as I walk into the kitchen where she's sat with her head in an interior design magazine, waving her hands around—presumably trying to dry her nail varnish. I pull out a can of Coke from the fridge before continuing. "I've taken the litre bottle of vodka from the drinks cabinet, and I've got a pack of condoms... you know, just in case." I lean back against the counter and watch for a reaction. *Any* reaction.

"Uh huh."

"I'm pretty sure some of the boys are bringing ecstasy."

"Hmm..." She hums as she turns a page and studies the room pictured.

"Didn't you only have a manicure yesterday? Why are you painting your nails already?"

Now, that gets her attention. Her head snaps up the moment the words 'nails' and 'manicure' leave my mouth. Surprise, surprise; my mother cares more about that than about alcohol, drugs, sex...and me.

"Yes, I did, but I just couldn't find a thing to wear tonight."

I doubt that's actually true, seeing as she's recently turned my eldest brother's old room into her personal wardrobe after already filling her own walk-in. "So, I went to that little boutique in town this morning and found the most perfect dress. Your dad will love it, but it didn't match the colour I chose for my nails yesterday."

"Wow, what a disaster," I mutter as I leave the room. "I'll be going out in about an hour. *Not that you really care*." I say the last bit quieter, but I'm not sure why; when I look back, Mum is once again too engrossed in her magazine to acknowledge me.

I let out a huge breath and head back up to my

room to finish packing for the party. I'm getting ready with my best friend Hannah and her twin Emma, who live next door. We've all been friends for as long as I can remember. Being twins, Hannah and Emma are really close, but Hannah and I are not far behind. The three of us do almost everything together; their parents have often joked that they have triplets, really.

I always laugh along.

Even though they know what my life is like, I don't think any of them really appreciate how much I wish that were true.

I'm just shoving my fourth outfit choice for the night into my bag when I hear my brother downstairs, greeting Mum. She instantly responds to him, which makes me laugh to myself, although it's anything but funny. One of her golden boys has come to visit. I bet if he needed something, she'd ruin that new nail varnish in an instant. God, I can't wait to get out of this hellhole I call home.

"Is Molly still here?" Daniel asks.

Her reply sounds suspiciously like, "I have no idea."

Walking to the other side of the room, I rest my hands on the windowsill and blow out a long breath as I gaze out over the countryside, trying to calm myself down. I keep telling myself not to get worked up by their actions, but sometimes it's easier said than done.

"Hey sis, I'm glad you're still here," Daniel says as he enters my room a few minutes later. My brothers are a lot older than me; I was an unplanned accident fifteen and a half years ago. Daniel is my youngest older brother and, at thirty years old, he's crazy protective of me. Steven is, too, but he now has a serious girlfriend so I'm seeing less of him these days. Daniel is my idol—always has been. He doesn't take life too seriously, does exactly as he pleases, works bloody hard, but always has fun. That's exactly what I want my life to be like, and I plan on making it so—once I get out on my own.

"Hey." I only manage one word because, as soon as I see him, I burst into tears. He pulls me into a tight hug. I hate that Mum and Dad can do this to me. Can make me feel so worthless. It makes me angry every time a tear falls for their actions. I wish I could be stronger.

"What have they done now?" Daniel asks. Both he and Steven know how our parents treat me. Hell, I couldn't count the number of arguments I've overheard about it on both hands and feet, but nothing ever changes. I'm just grateful that I have two amazing older brothers to turn to if I need to. Plus, I have my adopted family next door, who I'm pretty sure would do just about anything for me if I needed it.

"Nothing. I'm fine," I say, pulling away from him and wiping my eyes. I look at him and see the questions in his. "No, really; I'm just being a silly, hormonal teenager."

"Hmm...whatever you say, Molls. You still going to that party tonight?" I don't believe for a second that he buys my lie, but he knows it's easier for me not to discuss it. Nothing he can say is going to make any of it better, anyway.

"Of course, why?"

"I got you something." I watch as he reaches into his coat pocket and pulls out a small bottle of vodka before handing it to me.

"What's this for?" He looks at me and quirks an eyebrow. "I know it's to drink, you fool, but why are you giving it to me?"

"Because I remember what it was like being your age, and I didn't think anyone else would be buying you some. You deserve to act your age, Molly. Let your hair down. You work too damn hard trying to get your grades. But please be sensible. I don't want to be visiting you in the hospital or be an uncle yet. Actually..." He pauses as he reaches into his back pocket and pulls out his wallet.

My eyes widen in embarrassment. "No, no, no... I'm good, you don't need to worry about that."

I hate to admit it, but Daniel is the only one who knows what I've been up to. He let himself into my room one day while I was in my ensuite to find an open box of condoms on the bed and, being the protective brother that he is, counted them and realised two were missing. I'm hoping he doesn't want more of an explanation than that, because I really don't want to sit here and explain to my adult brother that I took myself off to the doctors a while ago and got myself on the pill—you know, just in case. Wouldn't that make Mummy and Daddy proud, to be grandparents while their daughter was still a teenager? Imagine the embarrassment.

"Okay, well, have a good time tonight, and ring me if you have any problems, yeah?"

"I promise."

I know I mentioned drugs and alcohol to my mum downstairs, but my group of friends isn't really into all that. I only said it as a way to provoke her in the hopes of getting some kind of reaction. Yes, there are plenty of kids at school who are at it every weekend, but my group actually cares about getting good grades and good jobs. The bottle of vodka Daniel just handed me will probably be it for us tonight.

"See you later then, kid," he says before kissing my forehead and leaving my room.

"THAT WAS AWESOME," Hannah squeals as the three of us stumble into the twins' bedroom sometime in the early hours of Sunday morning. Emma heads straight over to her side of the room and immediately starts replacing her party clothes with her pyjamas, while Hannah and I sit on her bed and reflect on the evening.

"So...come on, spill it...where did you go with Callum?" Hannah pleads.

"Just for a walk in the garden. I told you earlier!"

"I didn't believe you then, and I still don't now. I saw you two getting off with each other in the corner before you disappeared."

Callum is the boy at school that every girl dreams of. He's sporty, clever, funny and, of course, seriously hot, which is exactly why no one expected him to show his face tonight. But he did, and let's just say that I got to know him a little better than I did before. I'm yet to decide if that's a good thing or not.

"Will you two keep it down? I want to get up early tomorrow to do some coursework before we go to Grandma's," Emma complains from her bed.

Okay, so I said before that we work hard to get good grades, but Emma takes it to the extreme. I was actually surprised she gave herself tonight off. She's doing A-level maths already and does Spanish lessons after school to get herself an extra GCSE. I think she's putting too much pressure on herself, but she can't seem to stop in her quest to be the best accountant Oxford has ever seen.

"Sorry," we whisper simultaneously.

"So...come on, Molly, tell me," Hannah says, keeping her voice low.

I let out a frustrated breath and go for it. "Okay, so we went outside and found a quiet corner in the garden behind a bush. He pulled me down to the ground and we kissed for a while and let our hands... roam a little." I look up at Hannah and can see her excitement about what might come next.

"Oh my God, did you have sex with him?" she asks, but says the word *sex* much quieter. I don't know why; it's only Emma who could be listening.

"No, I didn't. I sorta thought we were going to, but by the time I got into his boxers, he was so worked up that he went off like a firework!" I can't help it, I burst out laughing at the memory, earning me another grumble from Emma.

"But I thought Callum's slept with loads of girls?" Hannah asks, confused.

"That's what the rumour mill says...I would be inclined to say that this was his first experience and the rumours are just that: rumours." We fall about giggling like the schoolgirls we are; I guess that vodka hasn't totally worn off yet.

"So, you *were* going to have sex with him, then?"

"Yeah, I guess," I say, shrugging my shoulders.

"But don't you want to wait until you're in love?" she asks innocently.

The only thing I have never told my best friend is that I lost my virginity last year at a party. Hannah has a different outlook on life thanks to her normal, loving family, and I don't want to have to explain my reasons for doing what I did that night—and a few times since. I totally understand her desire to wait until she's in love, and I admire her for it, but what I needed that night—what I *still* need—is to feel wanted by someone. And that first night? That was exactly how I felt.

FALLING FOR RYAN: PART ONE
CHAPTER ONE

Molly

Present

IT'S MIDNIGHT, and I've been sat on Ryan's doorstep for nearly an hour. I've already started on one of the bottles of wine. Although it was a scorching summer's day, the heat has now worn off, the clouds have gathered, and it's lumping it down with rain. I'm trying to tuck myself into his little porch to stop from getting so wet, but with the wind direction, it's not doing much good. I'm soaked through. It was a silly idea to pick white t-shirts when

I rebranded the coffee shop; thank God for padded bras!

By the time I'd cleaned and locked up, it was just gone ten. I love working at Cocoa's and have done so since I was sixteen. Hannah and Emma's parents own it. Susan started the business after she finished university. She came into some inheritance and, with the money, Cocoa's was born. The place was a huge part of my childhood. Hannah, Emma, and I would go there after school to do homework or just chat about boys, and it pretty much stayed that way until we finished university. We still have a booth in the back corner dedicated to us.

I will forever be grateful for Susan and her husband, Pete, whom she actually met as a customer in Cocoa's. It was love at first sight for them. Not only did they give me a job, but they took me under their wing when I was much younger.

Megan, who works in the evenings, had a phone call from her boyfriend at eight o'clock saying their little boy was really sick. I let her go home to be with him and finished up the rest of the night on my own.

Once I got in my car, all I could think about was having a nice hot bath and snuggling into bed in my tiny one-bed flat with my boyfriend, Max. We've been together on and off for the past three years, but when Hannah, whom I'd lived with above the coffee shop, decided eight months ago that she wanted her own boyfriend to move into the flat, I decided it was time I moved out and left them to it. Max had suggested I move in with him. I wasn't thrilled by the idea, to be honest, but at the time I didn't have the money to find anywhere decent to live. I hate being alone. I would have had to find someone who was renting out a room anyway, so it seemed like a sensible suggestion and a logical step in our relationship.

A week later, we all moved. Me into Max's flat, and Hannah's boyfriend into the one we'd shared for the past six years.

The ten-minute drive to our home seemed to take forever. I pulled up out the front; it was weird to be parking next to Max's car. He had worked nights the whole time I'd known him.

I dragged my body up the stairs to the third floor and let myself in. I shut the door behind me; the only light was coming from the bedroom. My heart dropped into my stomach when I heard voices and strange noises coming from down the hallway. As quietly as I could, I tiptoed towards them.

When I got to the door, I couldn't believe my eyes. Now, I knew Max was no angel, but I was under the impression that we had put the past behind us when we decided to live together and had become a monogamous couple. Yes, the past few months had been a strain, but still.

What was happening before my eyes on our bed showed me how wrong I was.

I numbly slipped back down the hallway and grabbed a couple of pairs of knickers that, luckily for me, were drying on the radiator, and left.

I tried to keep myself together as I made a pit stop at the shop on my way to Ryan's house. I didn't want to be one of those emotional women sobbing in the alcohol aisle, trying to decide which bottle would make me forget.

Once I'd paid for two bottles of my favourite wine and a crate of lager for Ryan, I made my way over to his new house. He'd only moved in two weeks ago, although it was months ago that he made the decision to buy the three-story townhouse in the new development on the outskirts of the city. It was basically a pile of bricks when he took me with him to see it for the first time, but I could see why he'd fallen in love with it. It was modern and spacious, with amazing views across fields from the back. From the front, you could see all the lights from the city in the distance. Because it was yet to be finished, it meant Ryan could choose a lot of the interior to suit his taste, and he didn't have to spend his whole summer re-decorating.

Grabbing my phone, I open up my messages to re-read the conversation I'd had with him earlier. He said he was going out tonight to celebrate the end of the school year but that he wasn't expecting to be home late. I guess that didn't really go as planned—not that he'd be expecting me to be sitting here waiting for him.

I'm starting to think I should have gone somewhere else. It's not that I don't have any other options, but out of all my friends and family, Ryan knows me the best.

What we've been through this year has made us close. I think I can safely say he's turned into my best friend somewhere in the last six months.

As I wait, images of what was happening on my bed flash though my head. I guess I should have seen it coming, really. A leopard never changes it spots, right?

Eventually, the tears come flooding out. To add to my misery, I now have black mascara streaks running down my cheeks and red puffy eyes.

Finally, I see headlights coming my way and Ryan's white Honda Civic pulling into his drive. At first, he looks shocked to see me. That changes to anger as he strides towards me.

Ryan

AS I COME TO A STOP, I can see that there's a very wet Molly huddled in my porch. She looks dreadful. I come to a very quick conclusion that it's because of her dickhead of a boyfriend. I knew it was coming; it was just a matter of when.

"Ryan," Molly sobs as I lift her tiny frame off the ground and into a hug. She shakes from both the cold and the sobs wracking her body.

Tucking her into my side, I grab her bags and let us in. On the ground floor, my townhouse has a large room with French doors looking out to the courtyard garden, and a bathroom. I thought it would make an excellent gym. The middle floor is an open-plan kitchen, living, and dining room with a small cloakroom, and the top floor has three bedrooms, one being the master with ensuite and the other a large family bathroom.

I love it.

From the moment I looked at the plans, I just knew it was going to be my little piece of heaven, and I'm still in awe that I was able to buy this place. I'll be forever grateful for the generous gift from Susan and Pete. Nothing will ever make up for what we all lost, but thanks to them, I've been able to attempt to move on with my life.

Currently, there are boxes everywhere. I haven't had much time to unpack with everything I had to do at school to end the year, but my first holiday job is to get this place sorted and looking like a home.

Anger fills my veins as I lead us up to the living room. "It's going to be okay. Let's get you warm and dry and you can tell me what the fucker did." My fists clench. I want to beat the shit out of him for treating her so badly for so long.

"How do you know he's done anything?" Molly asks in a quiet voice.

"I can read you like a book, Molly Carter. Plus, he's a massive dickhead. I think I've mentioned that before. Only Max can make you feel this bad about yourself."

"Why was I so fucking stupid? I had my doubts, everyone had their doubts, but he convinced me that it was what he wanted. I'm not really surprised, but what does shock me is how much it *hurts*."

"Come on, get your arse upstairs and in the shower. I'll find you a t-shirt to wear."

AS I ROOT through a suitcase in one of the spare bedrooms, the door to my ensuite shuts. I pull out my Oxford Brookes polo and leave it on my bed. I hope my choice will make her smile, remembering happier times.

I knock lightly on the door. "Have you got everything you need?"

There's silence for a few seconds, and I can imagine her checking out all the products in the shower, realising they're all for men. Eventually, I hear a quiet "Yes" from the other side of the door.

"Okay, I'll see you downstairs when you're done. Take your time."

I gather up her wet clothes and take them with me. They may be soaked, but I can still smell her vanilla scent on them. It makes me feel oddly warm inside. She's been my rock for the past six months. I don't know what I would have done without her.

As I put everything in the washing machine, I spot her bra poking out of the pile. "What the fuck do I do with this?" I mutter to myself. Something in me wonders if it needs some kind of special cycle in the machine, but fuck if I know. I decide to shove it all in and just put it on a cool, quick wash.

That shouldn't do it much damage, right?

DOWNLOAD NOW to continue reading